Delivery

Delivery

Emanuela Barasch Rubinstein

Holland House

www.hhousebooks.com

Paperback ISBN: 978-1-910688-93-9
Cover design by Ken Dawson Creative Covers
Typeset by Polgarus Studio

Published in the UK

Holland House Books
Holland House
47 Greenham Road
Newbury, Berkshire RG14 7HY
United Kingdom

www.hhousebooks.com

In memory of Jill Claster
My lifelong friend

The horseleach hath two daughters, crying Give give. There are three things that are never satisfied, yea, four things that never say not, It is enough: the grave; the barren womb; the earth that is not filled with water; and the fire that saith not, It is enough.

(Proverbs 30:15-16)

Afterbirth

Now that it is all over—life's first cry, the exaltations and tears of joy, the newborn baby taken to be weighed and measured, the stains of blood and amniotic fluid washed off, the narrow incision stitched, the sweat wiped from my forehead—a sigh of relief escapes me, almost against my will. In spite of the hustle and bustle, the midwives' lively conversation, a cleaner dipping a mop in a bucket and wiping the floor over and over again, a doctor asking for a senior colleague's advice, I feel silence enveloping me. No one is demanding that I breathe vigorously, that I strain my body to its very limit, or that I try, in vain, to stop a cry of pain. I am left alone, as if I were an old musical instrument that after much effort has made an ancient sound and now is placed back in its case.

Amir has left the delivery room to call the family and tell them that a healthy baby was born. I hear his excited, somewhat cracked voice coming from the corridor; he adopts a practical tone but is unable to conceal its trembling. The baby's weight is almost three kilograms. When he came into this world the doctor turned him upside down and only then did he begin to cry loudly. Amir says he doesn't know who he looks like, probably both of us—only his skin is shrivelled and wrinkled like that of an old man, maybe because he remained in the womb two weeks longer than expected, and two hours without amniotic fluid. Amir hastened to end the call and now he is phoning my parents, repeating the description of the birth, not leaving out the slightest detail. It is already a script that he has learned.

I am lying in a maternity bed: my body is clean, the incision is covered with a bandage, but I can't move. A chill is spreading within me, like an invisible shudder, a final quiver of disfiguring pain. Something is vibrating within my feet, advancing towards the bleeding wound, passing the abdomen and going up, intermingled with rapid heartbeats, making my breathing heavy. My body is rebelling. I close my eyes, thinking: here, it is all over, the pain is gone and all that is left of it is residual bleeding; but my dizziness proves that it cannot simply be swept away in an instant. The room is clean and sterile, the strong lights are turned off, I am wrapped in a pleasant blanket, the nurse brings me water, and I hear the staff saying that the room should be vacated as another woman in labour is coming. I find it hard to grasp how the heavy burden has suddenly disappeared, and all I have is a wordless memory of pain, a sensation fierce and acute that now only stings.

Amir returns to the room, looking at me with concern. He comes to my side and begins caressing my hair. "Relax, everything went well, the baby is fine, everything is okay." In spite of his casual tone he is looking anxiously at the lights, at a pack of towels at the side of the bed, at the syringes placed on a shiny tray; he stretches out a hand and grabs a bottle filled with pink fluid, grasping it and then putting it back on the tray; his hair, speckled with grey, is slick with sweat; his tee shirt is wrinkled and stained; he is staring at the walls like a boy who is made to spend time with a distant aunt, seeking to conceal his desire to run to the entrance, to be gone without waiting for the door to close. But he remains seated, and even tries to have a conversation.

After a couple of minutes he caresses my head again, and then says quietly, as if conveying a secret, "I'm going to see the baby." Here, finally, a serious excuse has been found, something that would not appear as a pretext but as a valid and important reason for him to kiss me and leave the room. The way he looks at the entrance is so obvious, I'd rather he would simply say: *Daphne, I can't take this place anymore, I must get out.* But he insists and lingers for a while before walking out, at first hesitantly, then with an appearance of justified decision.

A loud scream comes from the corridor: a woman shouting "I can't take it anymore, I can't take it anymore." Two nurses rush into the room. They cover me and roll the bed away. "6cm dilated, the room has to be readied quickly, she'll be in active labour soon."

I hear them talking as they push me into another room, placing the bed next to the window before rushing to the woman who has just come in. Isolating silence fills this room, and the screams of horrid pain cannot be heard here.

*

Finally, the labour is over. I can't stand this room for another moment. Though the blood has been completely wiped away, and all those repulsive fluids discharged by the human body have been cleaned up, and the stained towels have already been tossed into a bag, Daphne is lying in bed with eyes closed and I am eager to get out, to walk quickly through the corridor, to pass the cafeteria at the entrance of the hospital and, at last, step outside. God, how I long for some fresh air.

3

I thought I would choke in that room. Her painful cries are still present there, the awful yelling that turned into a choked weeping between long, strangely frightening bouts of heavy breathing. The midwife took the baby, wrapped in a towel, and the doctor left the room, but I find it hard to believe that all this unbearable pain has simply faded and disappeared.

Daphne opens her eyes. Softly she asks where the baby is and pats my wrist, looking at me distantly. Fleetingly I think I see a spark of despair in her eyes.

"In a minute the nurse will bring him back," I answer, thinking that if the infant were here I would not be able to leave. I sit beside her: her dark red hair looks almost black, perhaps with sweat—sweat covered her, rolled down her forehead, her eyebrows, her cheeks.

I find it hard to sit next to her now. During the pregnancy I felt there was something cheerful and inviting about the curved stomach, the growing and expanding body. Even though her belly kept protruding, I found the welcoming roundness apparent also in the softening of her facial features, the beautiful full breasts, the smooth arms that no longer had a virginal appearance; even in the slightly swollen legs.

But now she seems empty. I try to talk, but I keep looking at her body, thinking she is hollow, that all that filled her is gone. Her face, which always had a healthy glow, is now pale and bluish. And her stomach, which now I realize had stretched immensely to carry the baby, is destroyed and sunken. Her legs, still swollen, are unmoving on the bed—and in her eyes (I can't look at them but only glance now and then) a desperation I have never seen before. She says I can leave, that she wants to rest, but her little smile reveals a new agony. Though I am eager to leave, my hand stretches out and caresses her hand.

"Come on, Daphne, it's all over," I say.

My words surprise me, it is strange to speak of the birth of a healthy, first-born son as an end. I was expecting relaxation, to sigh with relief, but now I miss the tense anticipation of the contractions. An unexpected gloom is taking its place. Perhaps Daphne is waiting for me to hold the baby, to kiss him? I am eager to cross the room and leave. Out there, in the clear air, perhaps what is spreading within me would withdraw and disappear. It is as if what was removed from Daphne is now becoming part of me, heavy and oppressive, taking the place of the boundless joy that I thought should have filled me.

First Month

A strong scent of blossom was coming from the yard. I sat in the old armchair on the porch, my eyes closed, my head against the high headrest. Birds chirped from the tall oak tree; a light, almost imperceptible, breeze moved its branches and the leaves rustled softly. I could hear the voices of boys in the distance, perhaps quarrelling, but they faded away quickly. Our porch, on the first floor, faced a backyard surrounded by trees, concealing the houses down the road and the narrow alley between them. In the peaceful darkness I could pretend it was a country home with wide meadows stretching away behind the trees. The night wind was free from remnants of car exhaust and urban dust; the air was saturated with a pleasant coolness, enveloping the trees and the plants.

I thought that if I closed my eyes this day would vanish, as if it had never happened. The intense excitement, the hugs, the display of joy, Amir's whispering into the phone, which I overheard from the porch, and an inexplicable anxiety, slowly materializing and turning into a physical stress that I couldn't ignore—they would all fade away if I didn't open my eyes. Yesterday evening, at this hour, everything was as usual, a daily routine unfolding as expected. A young couple, newlywed, wanting to bring a child into this world. Everything was progressing normally, according to plan. But something went wrong. I don't know what it was. I find it hard to understand what happened, how this joyous event was transformed into a preposterous burden that I can't push aside.

All those smiles, Amir's tight hug as he said arrogantly: "Well, I did take care of things, didn't I?" only deepened the gloom. The kiss he demanded, long and straining; his eyes bright with joy; his excited brisk pacing back and forth, repeating over and over again that "we shouldn't tell everyone yet": they all seemed ridiculous. But still I smiled, yielding to his affection, pretending I was part of it. Frankly, I would have liked to lie in bed, pull a blanket over my head and sink into deep sleep. I would have liked to pretend that the nurse had never called and said she was happy to let us know that the result was positive, that I am pregnant; to pretend that I never beckoned to Amir to come to the phone, that he didn't ask to talk to her, just to make sure it was not a mistake. I laughed out loud, as if I had heard a funny joke, and Amir looked at me with surprise and suspicion and asked why was I laughing.

"I don't know," I replied, suppressing an inappropriate roar.

When the excitement was over, after hugging me, Amir started to offer me a glass of wine but then changed his mind saying it wouldn't be wise to drink now. I simply walked to the porch and plopped into the huge armchair. I closed my eyes hoping that all this would turn out to be a silly joke, something frightening and then funny. But after a couple of moments of silence, although I kept my eyes closed and listened to the nocturnal sounds, the pregnancy gradually materialized: I am pushing a stroller, I am changing diapers, I am bringing the baby to my parents, my stomach is becoming rounded, my clothes don't fit me anymore, I need to buy new dresses, I am nauseous, I am vomiting, and then, *my god*, a terrible fear takes over and won't go away, I am brought to the delivery room, pain distorts my body, I am screaming, my body is torn.

I opened my eyes.

"Daphne, are you okay?"

"Yes."

"Would you like to drink something? I mean, some water, perhaps." I guessed he was wondering if I was allowed tea or coffee.

"No."

"How are you feeling?"

"Fine."

"You don't look happy. Are you sorry you're pregnant? Would you like us to wait before we have a child?"

"No."

"You do want children, don't you?"

"Yes."

Amir returns to the room, leaving me staring into the shadowed world, my eyes following the night birds springing up with a cry and soaring to another branch. The trees look still, but an observant eye detects thin branches moving slightly, shaking their leaves. I close my eyes again, attentive only to my body. Where is the embryo now? A terrible fear, which I always knew existed but whose acuteness I only now understand, erupts, and there is no way to stop it. The understanding that a living creature will grow and develop within my body and then break its way out is petrifying.

*

When the phone rang I stopped myself from running to take the call. I sat at my desk, waiting for Daphne to answer. If she hadn't been at home I would have rushed to the phone, but I didn't want her to see how eager I was to find out if she was pregnant. Since early morning I have tried to be near the phone, to answer quickly, every ring sparking excitement; I knew the results of the pregnancy test would come through today. At eight o'clock Daphne's mother called, asking if we already knew. She always provokes anger in me, but I restrained myself and answered politely "no, not yet." As soon as I hung up the phone rang again. A woman, not young from the sound of her voice, was trying to persuade me to purchase tickets to a local theatre. Again I replied politely, feeling my pulse returning to its normal rate, once more eager to conclude the conversation quickly. I sat at my desk, papers before me, my fingers rolling a pen. My left leg trembled involuntarily. I listened to the sound of running water in the bathroom as Daphne took a shower, envisaging her naked body with drops of water running down it, an elongated yet curved figure, long, wavy red hair, huge eyes, probably closed now, and her mouth slightly open.

It was Daphne who took the nurse's call. After a couple of words she called me, crying out loud "it's positive." I asked to speak to the nurse, to double check that there was no mistake, to remove any doubt that Daphne is indeed pregnant. In a split second the expectation turned into cheers of joy. I thanked the nurse (after asking her a couple more times if she was absolutely sure it was not a mistake), and then turned to Daphne.

She looked a bit strange, bursting into wild laughter, and then halting, then stifling a groan. There was something horrifying about her laugh, the bestial, joyless sound of a wild animal. For a moment I thought there was something cruel about her countenance, but she suppressed everything and looked at me with those huge brown eyes, tossing her red hair forward onto her breast, and smiling sweetly. I hugged her tight. I wanted to kiss her, but a hidden movement within her body betrayed resentment. Still, I insisted. The happiness that filled me, a childish wish fulfilled, made me need to kiss her deeply, determinedly.

I told myself she must be tired, pregnant women are always exhausted, surely all this tension created fatigue. But a feeling of loss took over: something I thought would overflow and erupt is now retreating and sinking. Daphne's slight withdrawal, her instinctive recoil, and her hurrying to the porch, left me walking to and fro in the kitchen, wondering whether I should follow her or leave her alone. Yet my feelings remained unchanged: immense childish pride, something that simply must be shared. I grabbed the phone, trying to keep as far as possible from the porch, and called Guy.

His husky voice soon answered. In spite of the deep tone I heard a child, my friend from primary school. "Daphne is pregnant," I whispered, hoping that he would hear me and not ask me to repeat it more loudly. Silence fell. For a moment I thought I had failed and Guy hadn't heard me, or perhaps that he wasn't sure who was calling. I stood at the far end of the kitchen, next to the window, my head almost sticking out, waiting for him to break the silence, expecting a burst of greetings. After a couple of moments of silence I said "Guy?" and then came the greetings. He kept saying "well done," asked how Daphne was feeling, how her family is taking it, and when I said we hadn't told them yet he laughed loudly, and said it's better this way. Unclear voices came from the background. Guy said he was working, we should talk when he finished, when he got home, and he said once more "well done," and again silence fell.

Daphne slept through the day. When I suggested that I call

the family, she waved from the bed, indicating that I should not bother her. At night she got up to eat, and afterwards sat in the big armchair on the porch, looking out without saying a word. Something about her silence, the forced smiles, her head back against the chair, provoked my anger; yet I was careful to conceal it.

But my urge to celebrate a triumph wouldn't go away. Finally a desire to show something (though I wasn't sure exactly what it was) made me call our parents. Mine were full of joy, this would be their first grandson or granddaughter. My dad almost cried as we spoke, and mum was laughing quietly behind him, making a list of things that must be prepared: a cradle, nappies, a stroller, as if the baby was about to come into this world in a couple of minutes, and we had to hurry to purchase everything. Their choked voices brought tears to my eyes, and the triumphant feeling was gone, replaced by an annoyingly sentimental mood. Daphne's parents were happy, but her mother immediately explained that an eighth grandchild is not as exciting at the first, they were already used to it, and then she began a long description of how Daphne's older sister gave birth: they were so anxious they couldn't sleep and in the morning when their granddaughter was born they were so exhausted they could hardly celebrate. Her account of other pregnancies twisted over and over, now it was about their second, and now third grandchild, and so Daphne's pregnancy became merely a chapter in a long and tedious story, and I waited for it to end.

Again I went to the porch. Daphne was still sitting there, her head on the headrest, looking at the treetops, observing the night. I tried to hug her. She smiled, but again a hidden cord within her body stretched, an invisible movement of resentment. For a moment I was in a panic, perhaps she really

11

didn't want any children, or maybe not now, but she said with full confidence that she was glad she was pregnant and wanted a child very much.

I left her alone and went back into the room. Distress, anger, hurt were all unfolding and combining, and wouldn't dissipate. I walked into the kitchen and began to wash the dishes absent-mindedly. I placed the clean dishes and glasses on the dish rack, washed the cutlery. I cleaned the kitchen floor and then looked around, wondering how I could further tidy the house. I arranged the cushions on the sofa, tossed a biscuit packet Daphne had finished into the bin, threw a wet towel into the laundry bag—and then I saw the tiny glass cat Daphne likes so much. She bought it in Venice many years ago and had always placed it next to her bed, but now I was surprised to find it on a shelf in the living room. She must have moved it. I held it now. Its red moustache stood out against the transparent glass, its slanted eyes were glazed, its tail lifted, and I wanted to give it to Daphne. As I walked to the porch, holding the cat carefully, I called her but she didn't answer, and then I saw she was asleep. Even this small gesture was unwelcome, she had fallen asleep without saying a single word. Her legs were stretched forward, her hands placed on the armrests, her head turned aside, and her long hair fell down behind the high headrest.

For a moment I thought I would take her in my arms and carry her to the bed, but immediately I saw how ridiculous it would be, she would open her eyes and ask me to put her down, moving again the invisible part of her that pushes me away. Without hesitation I went quickly to the kitchen and throw the glass cat into the can. The sound of breaking glass didn't wake Daphne, only I was slightly taken aback by it. I fell onto the bed, covered myself with the huge blanket, and gave in to anger at being deprived of my joyous triumph.

Third Month

In the heat of the summer the buildings of Tel Aviv look scorched and dusty. At noon the sun turns into a blazing flood that penetrates everywhere. Street cats, normally sitting on fences and watching people go by, hide in the shadows, which they leave only briefly to find leaky garden taps. Shrubs bow their heads, trees adopt a yellow-green hue, vapours rise from the sea.

I am sitting facing the mirror, examining my bold new haircut: modern, clean-cut, pointed ends in the front and the back of the head. My black shirt balances my slightly juvenile face, pug nose, round cheeks, small eyes under light, curved eyebrows. I am not sure whether I should put on some make up; perhaps not. The need to beautify might be misinterpreted tonight.

Amir and Daphne are on their way to us. Ever since they told us Daphne was pregnant there was a special urge to invite them, as if we should accept the pregnancy as part of our lives. Two weeks ago Guy called and invited them. In a breaking voice Amir apologized, said Daphne was very tired and practically couldn't get out of bed. He added that when she returns from work she stretches out on the couch, sleeping in spite of the loud voices coming from the TV. He could hardly get her to move to the bed. We invited them again, but Amir had to stay late at work. Guy called time and again, and tonight they are finally coming to visit us.

I've just finished cleaning the living room: I tossed clothes scattered on the floor into the bedroom, cleaned food leftovers from the day before, and placed the dirty cups in the dishwasher. The pile of newspapers under the table was so heavy that I couldn't carry all of it to the trash in one trip. I even tried to remove a stain from the rug, but the more I scrubbed it the more it spread. I placed the colourful cushions on the sofa, wiped the glass coffee table, removing circle stains of coffee mugs and wine glasses. I then opened the window wide, hoping the fresh air would remove what seemed to me the musty, heavy smell of a dark closed room.

After a last glance round, I took a quick shower. I was standing facing the wardrobe, wrapped in a pink towel, as drops of water were falling on the floor, wondering what I should wear. Habit made me reach out and grab the black shirt, a soft shiny fabric that fits my figure very well, but I remained motionless in front of shelves loaded with expensive clothes. I have never stood like that looking at the open closet, unable to choose what I should wear. Guy always says that I dress faster than he does. My clothes match each other; I can easily choose a dress, or pants and shirt, which seem to be made specially to cover my body. But tonight I stood frozen in front of the wardrobe, trembling and slightly confused, unable to decide what to wear.

Finally I took a step forward, turning to the mirror on the inner side of the wardrobe door. I dropped the towel and examined my body, detached, almost curiously: short, but not too short, straight shoulders, arms slightly muscular, boyish breasts, too small, unbecoming to my bold look. The belly, which doesn't agree with very young looking breasts, betrays a fullness I am trying to conceal. Rounded thighs, in spite of exhausting training, the lower part of my body doesn't fit the upper part, as if a young, mischievous girl was attached to a full figured woman. For a moment I wondered – if I were pregnant, would the two parts of my body become congruous, would the dissonance transform into perfect harmony? But immediately I pushed away the disturbing thought, put on a tight black shirt and black trousers, then decided not to put on any makeup. The clean face should look innocent, remove misleading speculations on my decision not to have children.

When I told my mother I didn't want to have children she said nothing. I thought she would protest, even if in a feeble tone, but she, sitting at the table, immersed in contemplation, looked at me almost with understanding. Widowed years ago when I was a child, she tried not to share her sadness with me. Though my needs were always satisfied, for my father had left us plenty of money and we lived very comfortably, still sadness always coated her face, even when she laughed. Since I was an only child I hesitated before telling her I didn't want children; when I did she didn't seem surprised, as if she had anticipated this. Her indifference almost insulted me, but immediately I came to my senses, thinking it was better this way. I would have found it hard to resist if she had urged me to have children. Whenever she asked me for something, always quietly and softly, I couldn't refuse. Her implicit pain created a need to gratify her, to make her smile, however fleetingly.

That day when I told her we sat in the kitchen, the seashore of Tel Aviv was visible from the window, crowded with families sitting together on the hot sand, children playing and jumping all around them, laughing out loud. At this evening hour the sea was quiet, a huge canvas sheet spreading into the distance with a golden stain in its heart. Mum gazed with detachment, and said: "Abigail, the only thing that I care about is that you'll be happy. Nothing else matters."

And so the fact that I didn't want to be a mother had been established, accepted, made official, creating a pleasant sense of freedom. We both looked at the seashore: some people were boisterous, others were lying motionless near the sea that touched them and then pulled back. Mum stroked my arm, again creating a need to cheer her. I suggested we go to a good restaurant and she agreed immediately, almost with relief.

Dan, my partner at the time, was surprised when I told him about the conversation with Mum.

"Strange that she takes it so easily," he said, caressing my head after we had slept. "Doesn't she want grandchildren? And in fact, why don't you want to have children?" He found it bizarre that an attractive woman like me, always courted by men, was giving up a desirable development without a plausible reason.

"I don't know, I simply want to do whatever I wish, without thinking of nappies and babysitters." I didn't clarify any further, in spite of his questions about marriage and family. There was no way to describe the need to turn inwards, to indulge in anything that was intended to gratify no one but myself. I knew my explanations would appear petty, as though very little effort was needed to concoct them, and I insisted on avoiding it. But by then I had already realized that I lacked any desire to be a mother.

After that evening Dan had begun testing me, as though I

was concealing a secret he wished to discover. When we passed by children in the street he would point at a one of them and say "Cutie, ah?" waiting in anticipation for my response. He was curious whether I liked to cook, and was surprised to find I cook well, rather enthusiastically. When his nephew was born he invited me to the *brit*. I declined the invitation. There was something overbearing about these questions, even though they seemed to be uttered innocently. They were repeated constantly, in various forms. One night I woke up in his bedroom, looking at the ceiling, the chandelier, the windows, and decided I would leave and never return.

"Abigail!" came a cry from the door. Guy had arrived home and was surprised to see the room so tidy. "I don't recognize our house," he said, smiling. He had bought a bag of fresh pastries, which he placed in colourful bowls on our coffee table. Then he began to fuss over their arrangement. At first, he laid them in a row. Then, after hesitating, he made a square out of the four of them. Finally, he changed his mind, and placed them one next to the other. He then brought glasses from the kitchen and put them on the table, and finally moved the sofa a bit, so it stood at a perfect angle to the armchair next to it.

When Daphne and Amir came, we were all embarrassed. She looked peaceful, though tired and pale. She sat very carefully on the armchair, stretching a hand to the armrest before letting her body down onto the chair. Amir immediately began talking about the pregnancy, as though there was no point in a conversation about anything else: the doctor appointments, the equipment that should be purchased, the risks of the delivery, the various stages of the pregnancy. In spite of his light, sometimes funny, tone, there was something oppressive in the room, a looming presence, as if another person, invisible, was there with us. To defuse the tension I offered food and drink, behaving like an experienced housewife entertaining young relatives. I would have gladly brought my favourite red wine—drinking it straight from the bottle—and listened to loud rock music. But Guy said we shouldn't offer wine, not now, so I was left holding a glass of orange juice, coaxing Daphne and Amir to have some food.

To my utter surprise Guy began to ask Amir about various details of the pregnancy, how long it is, when could one think of the foetus as a baby, at what point does it have a heart, when is it possible to tell whether it is a boy or a girl, until what stage is an abortion possible, what actually happens during the delivery. Guy and Amir were immersed in this conversation, as if the pregnancy was a riddle to be solved; a process that could only be understood if it were broken up into small parts and clarified by fully predicting it. They were talking as if it were the embodiment of perfect health.

Guy said that the process of human reproduction is very interesting, and the small details are fascinating, and it's strange that, generally speaking, everything unfolds properly, since there are so many complex steps.

Amir replied, "I also thought it was pretty simple. Animals reproduce in nature. But now that I think about it I see how many things can go wrong."

I found Guy's extreme interest in the pregnancy strange. He seemed to be envisaging every step in the foetus's development. If he hadn't been so fascinated by these depictions I would have suspected that he was pretending, trying to please his childhood friend. He stretched out on the sofa, his muscular body loose, his feet turned outward a little.

His curly hair was leaning against the headrest as he stared into the room, imagining a growing embryo. I have never seen him like that, I thought. In spite of his muscles and a somewhat coarse skin, a result of running for hours along the seashore, he was as flexible as a young girl. But now, relaxed on the sofa, there was something sluggish about him which I had never seen before; the slack arm on the arm rest, the neck that looked slightly fuller, a sandal that had come off one foot.

Daphne sat quietly, smiling, pretending that she was following the conversation. When they burst out laughing she joined them, but it was clear she was lost in her own thoughts, and that she found the minor practical details of the pregnancy irrelevant. When I cleared the dishes she followed me to the kitchen. I asked her how she was feeling, and she replied she had never been so tired. She stood next to the door, leaning against the wall, sweeping her long hair back. Unintentionally I looked at her abdomen, smooth and shapely. For a moment I wanted to caress her, to run my fingers softly through her long hair, perhaps even touch her smooth cheek, but I stopped myself.

"Daphne, what's it like to be pregnant?"

"I'm tired, nauseous, and everyone is telling me what to do."

"Why don't you just rest at home?"

"It's impossible to rest. The problem is inside me."

I observed her in silence and didn't know what to say. She smiled at me and said quietly: "I want a child, that's all."

In an instant my patience was gone: I wish they would leave, I can't stand them anymore. All those exhausting descriptions of a foetus developing into a human being; the tedious observations about what is happening within

Daphne's body, as if we are all witnessing a miracle, and if we don't look closely it will disappear, I couldn't take it anymore. I rinsed the dishes angrily, tossing the plates into the dishwasher, avoiding Daphne. She turned and walked away. Enough—all this useless effort to reconstruct a normal, ordinary process is turning into a nuisance. I broke a glass and picked up the pieces, ignoring loud questions from the living room. Daphne and Amir made a hasty farewell, thanking us but saying they were very tired, Amir had to get up early tomorrow. They quickly closed the door behind them.

As I heard the door close I left the sink and the dishes and finally took the bottle of red wine, poured a full glass and drank it with pleasure. Ah, how I had longed to sip this wine, to stop pretending that I have any interest in this pregnancy, to ignore Guy's strange urge to make it part of our life. And his laxity, which I saw for the first time, as though only by coincidence had he turned out to be the curly-haired, tanned young man who likes to run on the Tel Aviv beach more than anything, was shocking. I always thought that the sweet, childlike smile peeking out of his sweaty face and wild hair revealed an utter surrender to the breeze wafting from the sea, pushing him from behind in one direction of the run, and slowing him on his way back. And his habit of taking off the running shoes after the run and rushing into the water—it was impossible to imagine that he could ever relax on the sofa in that way, his body adjusting to its angles, discussing with his best friend the various stages of an embryo's development in the uterus.

I poured myself another glass of wine, its bitterness creating a feeling of being asleep while awake, and went to the living room. I thought I would make up for this evening,

I would turn off the light and take off Guy's clothes, his eyes would be closed and his mouth smiling. I would turn back to take off my clothes, knowing that he was watching me. But as I walk into the living room I found him sound asleep on the sofa, his arm dropped to the floor, and he was breathing heavily.

*

At five o'clock in the morning, when it is still dark, the air is saturated with a foreign wind; you might have thought it was not the Mediterranean seashore, but somewhere in Europe, in a chilly place. A dust-free breeze, transparent and delicate, leaves tiny water drops on the enormous philodendron's hand-shaped leaves at the entrance to the building. The street is empty, but a faint sound of rattling wheels, like a cart with rusty hinges, is always heard from around a blind corner. A cat leaps on its prey, and the twitters of night birds echo in the air. The tall trees are dark and motionless, the streetlights are still on, casting pale light filtering through the highest branches.

The first steps are always the hardest. The smell of the warm bed after a night's sleep, Abigail's hair on the pillow, the steaming morning coffee with plenty of extra milk, the unlit house full of yesterday's breath—every morning they create hesitation: should I run, or perhaps skip it for today? But the tension spreading within me, the alertness preceding physical effort, removes the homey comfort and makes me leap down the stairs, hurry from the building, and I begin to run in the direction of the sea. My feet are stiff, the knees bend under my body's weight. After a couple of minutes I reach the seashore, and the air, which at this early morning hour is somewhat heavy, unties an inner knot, making me run faster.

The shore is almost empty; the sea dark and cool. I see old men exercising, raising their arms upwards, to the side, and bending down. Bikes pass by me swiftly, other joggers struggle with the urge to pass one another rather than get drawn into a fixed inner rhythm.

After my breathing steadies, my body relaxes, and it is here that extra vigilance is needed: a thread unfastens, thoughts burst out, sometimes threatening to interrupt the steady motion of the legs. When I think of last night an unpleasant feeling spreads within me, though I don't really know why. Our house, unrecognizably tidy, the wide-open window, the refreshments on the coffee table, it all seemed like a façade, a set for a show that we are all taking part in: Daphne and Amir arrive, Amir drops on the sofa and Daphne sits very carefully, as if a sharp movement would be dangerous, Amir begins his explanations about the pregnancy, Abigail walks back and forth to the kitchen, acting like a housewife, offering food and drink to visitors, and we are all behaving in accordance with some obscure script.

I never imagined the process of a pregnancy could be so interesting. Amir's detailed description of the creation of a microscopic body of life, slowly developing a pulse, a sex, a nervous system, and becoming human, was fascinating. My dad used to say that pregnancy was the misfortune of women, thank god that we, men, don't have babies, and that it is better to stay away from them during pregnancy, since they are too aggressive. Years ago, while sitting in a fashionable coffee shop in Tel Aviv, waving at people passing by, he told me his secretary was pregnant. It was the way he said it, with a loud laugh and a wink at the waitress he was leering at, that made it sound as though pregnancy was merely the undesirable consequence of sex. Even the overtly masculine posturing, with his legs spread apart and his hand on my back, made any interest in what happens within the female body utterly preposterous.

Now I pass Tel Aviv's old port. The many restaurants and coffee shops, open until late at night, are now closed, though pale light is peeping out of some of them. Probably the cleaners haven't finished their work. I hate this part of the run. Here the sea is only a background to the wooden promenade and the fancy shops. Even the primordial smell of the sea mixes here with remnants of restaurants' smoke and alcohol. But I pass by them quickly, my breathing a bit more laboured, and I advance northwards.

About two years ago Abigail told me she didn't want to have children. I looked at her amazed, but without any hostility. In bed the night before we moved in together, she lay on her back staring at the ceiling, and said: "Guy, I want to tell you something. I don't want to be a mother."

When I asked why she replied: "I want to enjoy life, to experience many things—but not to take care of someone else."

At the time I thought her words were immature, so I insisted: "But what if you get pregnant? What would we do?" She turned her back to me, and I couldn't see her face when she said, "I won't change my mind."

I closed my eyes, repeating the words without fully grasping them. I was occupied with a plan to renovate an old house, wondering how I could please the boss and make the old building appear clean and modern; as the lead architect it was weighing on me, occupying my thoughts all the time. Thus Abigail's words were left unanswered, sinking in and disappearing without creating turmoil, without leaving the slightest ripple. But now, when Amir is about to become a father, they re-emerged, transforming into an obscure burden. Suddenly, it is as though something has been stolen from me; as though I never noticed its presence but now all I can feel is its absence. I feel cheated and betrayed.

I finally reach the Tel Baruch beach. Another small hill, here I turn around and begin to run back southwards. The wind, which slowed me down on the way here, is now pushing me forward, and I run faster downhill, again towards Tel Aviv's old port. The light dawning from the east doesn't quite illuminate the sea but gives it a metallic tone, while the mists coming from the west are coloured in strong orange and pink. The seashore is dim, but the curving path along the coast is brighter. I pass the old port and continue running southwards. When I am about to finish my run my breathing becomes very heavy, and I have to work hard to suck in sufficient air. One stride and another. I see my shoes moving forward at a steady pace, the sweat is dripping off my back, another moment, and then—

I remove my shoes and socks, and walk slowly into the sea. The seashells slightly scratch my feet, the water is cold, gentle waves engulf me, I close my eyes and surrender to the movement of the water. The shallow stream sways my floating body, and when I open my eyes I see that the sun has risen and bright light fills the sky.

Fifth Month

"May I help you?"

The shop assistant at the baby shop smiled at us, adopting the countenance of a nice grandmother. Amir and I had entered the shop hesitatingly, looking around at the merchandise: cribs, strollers, chests, bottles, toys in all shapes and colours—we didn't know which way to turn. The woman examined my oversized shirt with an astute expression, trying to determine how many months pregnant I was, and wondering, would it be wise to suggest the "delivery deal": a huge poster covering the entire window offered a bundle of products at a special price, pre-ordered and shipped immediately after the birth.

Amir took my hand and whispered, "Come on, Daphne, let's have a look at a couple of things, and then have lunch."

We slowly walked around the shop. Amir checked a couple of price tags with a grave expression—but when we reached the stroller department a smile crept over his face as he discovered something of an interest in this shop, all coloured in soft pastel tones. He started moving different strollers back and forth, checking the brakes, examining the handles, and suddenly the assistant was standing right behind us, though we never saw her approaching, smiling and saying "this is an excellent stroller," in a motherly tone, as if she were a relative who had come with us to the shop.

Amir inquired how much it weighed, how it folded, what the wheels were made of, and the woman immediately suggested another one ("a bit more expensive, but much better") and he followed her willingly, examining the technical details, comparing wheel size, the ratio between the wheels and the entire stroller, checking how each one reclined. I kept wandering around, staring at the white, gleaming cribs, the soft bedding, the variety of delicately decorated bottles, a baby carrier, nappy bags. Soft music filled the shop, a gentle xylophone seductively playing children's songs; the walls were covered with pictures of smiling babies. I walked on through the aisles, gazing from side to side, examining dummies, nappies, baby clothes, and, as I was pacing slowly, looking at the shelves, I saw a strange bottle whose purpose I couldn't figure out.

It was a transparent plastic bowl, like a thin eggshell already hatched, with a tap attached to the bottle. For a moment I thought a wine opener was stuck in a mouth of the bottle. But as I kept examining it, turning it from side to side, upside down, I saw a pink pamphlet next to it. The operating instructions. A smiling woman adjusted the bottle to a full, rounded breast, pumping breast milk into it, and above was a pretty red title: *Wouldn't you like your husband to get up at night?* I then realized that the shelf was full of pumps, some manual, some electric, pumping milk from the breasts of attractive women. A variety of bowls, attached to many breasts, sucking mother's milk to preserve it.

A hidden bubble gradually contracted within me. Its walls, thin yet durable, shrivelled, as if the air within it had been pumped out. I held my stomach, trying to halt the contraction, to stop the pain of the bubble cut off from the inner part of my body and turning into a hard, oppressive lump, but in vain. I bent forward, it was easier to take the spasm this way. I couldn't bear this shop any more, those weird pumps extracting milk from the mother's body, and the soft, pleasant products around me made me nauseous. The tunes playing in the background, the photos of smiling mothers with babies, it was all so sickening. For a moment I wondered why there was no picture of a screaming baby or of a dirty nappy.

I rushed to the door, and there stood Amir, smiling amiably, saying: "Where were you? I was looking for you everywhere. Let's have lunch." When he saw my distress he asked, "Are you okay?" and I nodded, eager to get to the restaurant and have something good to eat.

As we finally sat down at our table the nausea dissipated slightly, and I found I was hungry. A pleasant aroma filled the place, the chef was preparing the fresh dishes of appetizing looking Chinese food as the patrons watched. Amir wasn't sure what he wanted to have; he ended up ordering too many dishes, more than we could eat. Soon the table was full of small bowls filled with tasty food, and Amir seemed amused. He began describing the various strollers in detail, delving into their mechanisms, how they fold and unfold, the way the brakes work, and finally he asked: "Which stroller would you like to have?"

"I really don't know. Whichever you think is best."

"Come on, don't you care?"

"I honestly don't."

Amir examined me with curiosity, swallowed another chunk of beef, and said teasingly: "Still, if you had to make a choice…"

"I would buy the simplest one, undecorated, one that doesn't fold, isn't easy to carry, without any removable parts."

Amir laughed, though I was serious. "Why not make life a bit more comfortable?" he said, and then went on with a long explanation how new strollers are simply easier to use, they are made of lighter metals, more suitable for carrying a baby, unlike the heavy old carriages, which were so hard to push. As he was eating from various dishes, apparently still hungry, he kept on listing the advantages of modern materials, but I noticed that he was turning his gaze to the left, looking behind me. Embarrassment was gradually spreading over his face, though he kept talking as though nothing had happened.

"Hi, Amir. How are you?" I heard a feminine voice behind me.

I turned around and saw a handsome young woman, with light, straight hair, wearing a white man's shirt. She was smiling at Amir with utter confidence that he was happy to see her. There was something provocative about her countenance: her smile lacking any warmth, her green eyes bright, she was staring at me with slight contempt and asking Amir how he is doing.

He quickly introduced me, "Sari, this is Daphne, my wife," but his manner only emphasized his unease. The blush covering his face, his somewhat silly smile, like a boy caught in a mischievous act, the pragmatic tone he adopted—they both turned the conversation between them into a mutual pretence. He asked her whether she had completed her studies, where she lives; he brought up a couple of familiar names and asked if she had been in touch with them; she told some funny stories and Amir laughed loudly, all in order to conceal a secret they shared.

Once in a while she looked at me briefly, examining me closely, and then quickly diverted her gaze and smiled provocatively at Amir.

Again I felt the tiny bubble within me, but now it seemed to expand, to turn into a lump of clay, heavy and wet, almost bruising me. The food on the table seemed repulsive, noodles sunk in oily brown sauce, pieces of meat still dripping animal blood, a salad writhing with worms, it was all repulsive, nauseating. In a moment I would have thrown up on the table. Amir was looking at this woman with surreptitious desire, though attempting to adopt a merely friendly expression. The hints concealed in her words, alluding to past intimacy between them, were so obvious. I sat and watched them. My oversized shirt was slightly stained, my long hair dishevelled, resting on my chest, my arms were folded and my nails were digging into my arms.

After she bade us farewell and left, winking at Amir and smiling at me, he immediately began to explain: they had gone to college together, she is very smart, she did very well at university and went on to graduate school, very gifted, he always envied her for doing better than he did on tests. His ridiculous effort to adopt a casual tone, to believe that he could disguise their intimacy was so silly that I thought it useless to say anything. He kept describing the courses they took together, how, in spite of his obvious talent in mathematics, she did better than he did: every sentence carefully articulated, each word cautiously chosen to mask something so plain and obvious.

"May I have a glass of red wine please?" I asked a waiter passing by our table. He nodded, carrying a tray loaded with food to the next table. As I looked back at Amir I saw how his silly expression and bright eyes disappeared in an instant as signs of anger began to surface; his eyebrows were drawn closer, his features stretched and re-aligned, his mouth tightened, and his eyes moved restlessly from my face to the people around us, and then back to my eyes.

"Daphne, stop it. What's the matter?"

"Nothing, one glass of wine won't hurt."

"It won't help, either. Why don't you start smoking?"

I felt that here I had the upper hand. The anger he found hard to express, holding it within him until it breaks out in sarcastic remarks, hesitating over what he should do when the waiter comes with the wine... He kept turning the fork in his hand over and over again. His gaze travelled around restaurant, he was silent, looking embarrassed and angry, wondering whether he should firmly disagree or let me have the wine. As the waiter brought an elongated glass, almost full to the top, deep burgundy with a nearly invisible crown of bubbles, he folded his arms on his chest and spreads his legs forward, giving me a reproachful look.

"Cheers, Amir," I said, sipping the bittersweet wine with pleasure. He didn't answer, again his eyes moved from side to side. And then I said, "It's a shame you didn't tell me about your ex-girlfriend. She looks rather interesting. How long were you together?"

With one careless, sharp movement, Amir pushed a plate and it broke on the floor, the pieces spreading around the table. Everyone was looking at us, the waiters rushed to clean the floor, and in this bustle Amir was flushed, saying "You are out of your mind!" repeatedly, glancing at his ringing phone without taking the call, his jaws clenched and his muscles strained.

When I grasped the glass again and drank the wine he picked up the phone in a demonstrative manner, got up, careful not to run into the waiters who were still cleaning the floor and walked away briskly, almost running. For a moment I wanted to stop him, to apologize, to say I didn't mean to upset him, but just as he left the restaurant I saw him answer the phone.

I sat in the restaurant for two hours. I had a huge crumble cheesecake, chocolate mousse, and two more glasses of wine. My sight was blurred, I almost forgot that I was pregnant...

A devastating fear began to materialize, sometimes slipping and disappearing, sometimes as sharp as a broken bottle's neck. A terrible pain, unimaginable. My stomach hatches and a huge chick is coming out, dirty and featherless. I am placed on the maternity bed, bleeding and shocked, recalling the picture at the entrance to the baby shop: a beautiful woman with a broad smile holding a newborn baby whose eyes are closed.

*

Such bad luck, *God!* This is such bad luck! Tricks of fate, bitter-sweet. This lust, awakening the deepest human impulse, and here is my pregnant wife, carrying my son. Why did Sari happen to be in the restaurant, exactly when we were there? Why did she glance at me in her provocative way? Such bad luck. I wish we hadn't dined there. I wish it was yesterday morning, and all this had never happened.

As I go out to the street, an evening breeze moves the heavy leaves of Neem trees planted down the street. I find it hard to understand how I ended up here, how a day that began with a visit to the baby shop ended with me leaving Sari's house, my body exhausted, holding back the tears. What strange circumstances brought me here. Had we stayed in the baby shop for another couple of minutes, maybe had a prolonged conversation with the nice saleslady, or stopped to look at another window on our way to the restaurant, all this wouldn't have happened. My self-disgust is increasing since in spite of the repugnant image of my body on top of Sari's, a spark of self-satisfaction surfaces, the memory of conquest emerges for a moment before blending with despairing revulsion.

If only I hadn't answered the phone, if only I had let it ring in my pocket, I wouldn't be leaving her house and walking in this street with tears rolling down my face.

But it can't be undone.

Now I am thinking how I will return home and pretend that nothing has happened. For a moment a thought crosses my mind, perhaps I will tell Daphne everything—but immediately I realize how senseless that is. In no way will I allow my selfish desire to ease the burden of guilt to harm her. I wish I could rest my head on her shoulder and cry, but that's impossible.

And Sari, she is guilty too: gloating, smiling with false kindness. Even before I left the restaurant she called to say she was alone in the parking lot, so perhaps I could pop outside "to say hello." Her confidence that I was eager to see her, the slight, teasing smile, she made me stumble. At first I didn't see her in the parking lot (for a moment I thought she was fooling with me), but there she was, leaning against a blue car. As I walked toward her I wondered whether Daphne could see me through the window.

When I reached Sari she kissed my cheek and asked if I would like to have coffee. A beautiful, full figured woman, always wearing a man's shirt, her soft fair hair shining in the sunlight, her face creating the impression that she's keeping a precious secret, and she'll single out someone and whisper it in his ear.

A small fragment of shame was torn from its place, but I quickly pushed it away, telling myself there is nothing wrong with having coffee with her. The anger that was overflowing as I left the restaurant had subsided; Daphne's desire to have wine when pregnant was stupid and childish, it might be dangerous to the baby. And of course I didn't know Sari would be in the restaurant. Had I known, I wouldn't have come. Clearly Daphne was feeling uncomfortable, I understand that (I wouldn't have felt comfortable meeting her ex-partner). But her reaction was preposterous, why risk endangering the baby for that? As I think about it my animosity increases for a moment, and a sequence of arguments, structured and logical, is forming: her entire attitude to being pregnant is ridiculous, she is acting as though she is somehow being punished, instead of being happy about future motherhood. Her refraining from expressions of joy, her anger as she was told what she should be eating or drinking, her panicky look in the baby shop, it is all so silly, fitting a young girl and not a woman her age. One needs to prepare a cradle, a stroller, an armoire, nappies, bottles and many other things to bring up a baby properly, so what's the problem? How does she plan to raise the child, in a straw bed?

As I sank again into my anger I realized I was sitting in Sari's car and we were driving. I didn't ask where we were heading. Only when I observed that my left foot was shaking nervously did I stop thinking about Daphne and stare at Sari. Sitting facing the wheel, driving confidently, smiling at me she said: "You're looking good." There is something so arousing about her profile, long, light eyelashes, aquiline nose, such a provocative look, "Well, what's it like to be married?" she asked.

"It's a good life. I'm about to become a father in a couple of months."

"Really?" Surprise was spreading over her face, beginning with a slightly open mouth, traveling to a wild look in her eyes, and ending in an involuntary brushing back of her hair. She tried to conceal her disappointment. I don't know what she was expecting, but clearly she found Daphne's pregnancy awkward. She moved a little in the car seat, blew the horn at a car that came too close to us, and to disguise her discomfort asked: "How is your friend—I forget his name—Guy?" I smiled, stretched my legs and folded my arms. I tell her about Guy, Abigail, his job as an architect, and his jogging on the beach every morning.

An old memory, which I had almost forgotten, is gradually forming: Guy was eager to meet Sari, trying to run into her, and when he did, his face betrayed an unfamiliar embarrassment. But she mocked him almost shamelessly and unexpectedly wished to get to know me. I never thought it possible that a woman would prefer me over him. Guy was manly and muscular, a lady-killer, sometimes when his phone rang he looked at who was calling and blurted "stalker" without answering, but Sari was smiling at me, and invited me to her house. Guy seemed lost, his thin, pale childhood friend had suddenly become a competitor, he looked at me almost with hatred as I told him. I was sorry for him, but beating him was so intoxicating that I kept describing my date with Sari in great detail until finally he yelled "enough!", took his stuff and left my house, slamming the door, and I heard him leaping down the stairs, getting out of the building and beginning to run outside.

Sari seemed interested in my answers, examining every fact, looking as though she was memorizing my words, asking more questions, clarifying the facts, plainly, without any excuse. Why isn't Guy married to his girlfriend? When did I get married? Where do I live? What is Daphne doing? I tried to answer but I was absentminded, unable to collect my thoughts. I found the wine Daphne had so annoying, provoking a hidden bitterness. She behaves as though I have no part in the pregnancy, and if she chooses she could have as much alcohol as she wants, I am some kind of pest, insisting on trivialities. I suddenly recalled the phone conversation with Guy when I told him Daphne was pregnant, and wondered why he reacted so oddly. I felt a sadness beneath the manly tone.

Immersed in my thoughts I saw with surprise that we had stopped. Sari turned off the engine and pulled out the keys, ready to get out of the car. "Come," she said, "let's have coffee."

When I climbed the stairs my legs were shaking, almost as if I were awaiting punishment. We entered her apartment on the second floor, passing a neighbour who greeted us and looked at me with obvious curiosity. As we walked into the apartment I looked around almost with anger, wondering what kind of memory I would carry away. A beautiful Tel Aviv place, full of light, painted in bright white, with blossoming geraniums on the balcony. Sari waited for me to close the door and immediately wrapped herself around me, smiling in her enticing way, pulling me to the wide bed. Her small smile, the secret she never divulges, ignited a burning desire.

Even though Daphne is somehow present in the room—I feel her huge eyes following me, with amazement or pain, or perhaps she is leaning against the wall or collapsing onto a chair—I am too weak to struggle against this lust. When I am on top of Sari's body, as I see her nearly white eyelashes, the knot between my darkest desires and her fair skin glowing in the sunlight is fastened at once, and I collapse onto her chest, resting my head on her breasts.

When I left her house I had already swallowed my tears. I didn't answer her question, would I come again? I walked out of the dim stairway into the street, passing from interior gloom into the evening light. How can I return home? I walked down the street, kicking small stones on the pavement, purposely stepping on flowers in the park, tearing off an ad from a billboard. I stopped a taxi, got in, sat down, and asked the driver to take me to my parents' house.

As my mother opened the door, surprised to see me, smiling but then observing that something was wrong, I said, flustered,

"I am not sure Daphne and I will stay together. I am saying this so you won't be surprised."

The End of the Fifth Month

What a mess, God, what a mess. Such a strange, pointless outburst, a tantrum... I haven't heard my son Amir shouting like that for years, not since he was a teenager. As he did then, pale and thin, he now leans against the kitchen wall while I wash the dishes, uttering one accusation after the other, and I am unable to respond. What's wrong with him? Looking at me with burning eyes, defiant and insulting, mocking his father, as though he came for a visit only so we could quarrel.

As soon as he walked in he announced that he doesn't think he and Daphne will stay together, and that he is saying this so I won't be surprised. I stood at the door, hearing the words but unable to grasp their meaning. What does it mean they won't stay together? Only last Saturday they came for lunch, relaxed and smiling; Amir explained in detail how he thinks the baby's room should be arranged. Well, I had already been to baby shops, but obviously I said nothing. I listened carefully to his description, comparing every product he mentioned to the ones I had seen. Sitting like that, eating in haste while talking, I thought how good it was that he would become a father. His teenage gloom, perhaps a result of a constant sense of disappointment, had evaporated lately, and he had been eagerly anticipating the birth. But now, standing there while I washed the dishes, exactly as he did years ago, leaning against the wall with arms folded, shamelessly saying that his father and I are to blame for everything that has gone wrong in his life... and now he and his wife are about to separate before the birth of his first son, all because we implanted in him a profound fear of the birth and of caring for a baby.

Finally Aaron, the most gentle and patient father, couldn't take it anymore, and asked him to stop. "Enough. Mum and I did the best we could."

Amir flushed, he leaned harder against the wall, almost as though he was trying to push it. "Really?! I think you could have acted in a different manner."

I washed the dishes, one plate after another... placing them on the rack next to the sink. Since I had learned that Daphne was pregnant, bitterness began to taint my instinctive happiness. In an instant an old memory that I thought had faded over the years suddenly became clear and vivid, it seemed like only yesterday I gave birth to Amir.

When he called to say that Daphne was pregnant, for a moment I was cheerful, and joyfully I thought about all the things that must be bought, and how I would tell all my friends. But even before the call was over I was covered with sweat, as though I were feverish. I thought it was the result of the excitement, I didn't understand why my body felt like it was burning. Aaron and I hugged each other, he wiped his tears and I smiled, but for a split second, Amir's birth resurfaced. Hours of suffering, a delivery that went wrong and mutilated the mother, not the child, not the child, thank God... they all merged into a single vision that faded immediately.

Immersed in my thoughts I heard Amir's voice from far off, continuing to accuse me. "Anyway, you didn't hold me for almost an entire year, I am sure it affected me somehow. I understand it was a very difficult delivery, but surely it could have been treated somehow, you could have dealt with the problem. Don't you think a child is traumatized by a mother who can't hug him for a year?"

The memory returned again, as if thirty-five years hadn't gone by. The Ziv maternity hospital in Jerusalem spread in my mind... I felt as if I were in labour now. A wide hall with high ceilings, a strong smell of detergents, eight beds, equally spaced, awaiting women before labour, no decorations or pictures, I could feel the spirit of the Protestant Sisters who established the place. Aaron sat next to me for hours, refusing food in spite of the nurses' efforts; I felt they had more compassion for him than for me, that his expression provoked more empathy than my cries, which went on for hours. At first they dismissed my begging them to see what was going wrong as pure indulgence. A grave-looking nurse examined me and said everything was fine, all that was needed was some patience. I was lying hurting in bed... women who came after me were rushed to the delivery room before me. But after hours of tormenting pain I lost consciousness, and then doctors gathered quickly around me, calling a senior doctor in panic. Without advanced technology, they were trying to find out what had gone wrong. When I regained consciousness for a couple of seconds I saw Aaron looking at me, terrified, clutching his face, motionless.

"Did you try to discuss this with anyone? I am not sure the only reason was the trauma of the delivery," Amir said. For a moment I thought I saw a film of tears in his eyes, but he turned away quickly, and I saw his thin back and his hair, beginning to turn grey.

"Amir, I would like to explain, but it's so difficult to talk to you this way. Try to understand, your birth was very unusual, even at the time, and certainly today. In fact, the doctors made a mistake. They should have done a C-section without waiting so long. They risked both you and me, but the medical knowledge was different then." He didn't answer, and I thought it was an opportunity, a pause in this outburst of anger. "Those hours of suffering left me... I am not quite sure how to say this... indifferent to anything other than physical pain. The long hospitalization after the birth, the fear of anything that might create pain... Dad took such good care of you, allowing me to slowly bond with you, by choice. I made up my mind to become your mother."

Almost all the dishes were clean, only a couple of cups were left, a last pot waiting... Amir stood unmoving, absorbed in thought, still leaning against the wall but his body slightly relaxed. Perhaps this flash of memory, this moment that contained so many hours of pain, touched him. For an instant I thought he was present at his own birth: the street ascending from Jaffa Road to the hospital, the trees on both sides full of dust, the old building, beautiful but austere, so typical of the spirit of Jerusalem, the nurses who rarely smile, impervious to the screams of pain emerging from the maternity ward, the white bed sheet that had such a sour smell after a couple of hours, the horror in the young doctor's eyes as he tried to figure out what was going wrong, the contraction every thirty seconds, a barbed wire cutting my body from within, tearing the flesh, time and again, and then everything blurs, Aaron's face fades in a cloud, and tranquillity comes.

Amir was looking at me, his features somewhat softened, betraying a hint of compassion. Apparently he could envisage the sufferings of his own labour that materialized for a moment and disappeared. He lowered his gaze and said nothing. Finally he muttered, "Well, I should go. I'll say goodbye to dad."

*

"Dad, I'm leaving."

"Sit down for a moment, Amir. I don't want you to leave like this."

"I am so tired. God, I am so tired."

"Are you going home?"

"I don't know."

"Would you like to stay here for the night?"

"No. Not really."

"Shall I call Daphne and tell her you are staying here for the night?"

"No, Dad. Stop it. I can get along."

"What happened, son?"

"Drop it, Dad. It's personal."

"Amiri, can I be of any help? I see how hard it is for you."

"I am tired of this pregnancy, perhaps it's not right for me. I am sorry I yelled at Mum, but maybe it is a result of my revulsion about the entire process of giving birth."

"Well, I don't know what to say. In spite of the joy, this is not easy for us either."

"I didn't know it was so complicated: the pregnancy, the labour, and then taking care of the baby. I thought it would all happen naturally, but it doesn't."

"Well, I thought so too before you were born. Mum seemed so happy when she was pregnant. We never thought the labour would be so difficult, that it would turn into a burden, a trauma we would always carry. It all seemed so simple then. We used to believe that whatever happens in nature will unfold properly. If only we don't interfere with

41

this age-old process, everything will be fine. How wrong we were, God, it is hard to believe."

"Didn't you know that some labours go wrong?"

"Well, yes, in principle we knew. But we thought the natural process of reproduction has some profound wisdom, and that most medical interventions were unnecessary. When we went to the hospital as the contractions began—ah, it feels as though it happened yesterday—we went up Straus Street. Mum could hardly walk. It was a warm day, she was breathing heavily, and still she kept saying she wanted 'a natural delivery,' without anaesthetic. 'I want to give birth like my grandmothers did,' I remember her saying that. As we entered the hospital, gloom covered us, in spite of the beautiful building. Ah, the high eucalyptus trees casting shadows on it could be seen through the high, arched windows, and there was something serene about the wide hall, as if the women came here to fulfil a duty. There wasn't the slightest clue of the happiness the birth of a child can create."

"Maybe they were right, perhaps having children is a kind of duty."

"Amiri, Mum and I wanted you so much."

"Dad, drop it, I see how hard it is for you. Never mind, whatever. I didn't mean to bring up all these memories."

"They emerged anyway, from the moment you called to say Daphne was pregnant."

"I am sorry. I never knew that. I thought it was all forgotten."

"It was, but it still remained real and vivid deep down. Our lives completely changed after your birth. Mum was in the hospital for a couple of months. First in the gynaecology ward, then in the psychiatric ward. Hours of torment left her silent. Some things cannot be expressed in words."

"Why didn't you call someone? Cry out loud that you need help?"

"I called, explained, asked, yelled, begged. Finally I grabbed the young doctor's arm and began to cry, sobbing like a child, and only then was he willing to come and examine Mum. I stood there helpless, unable to ease her pain, seeing her accusing gaze, why wasn't anyone helping her? I am sure today this wouldn't have happened. It was an old hospital, and a different era. Today they would do a C-section quickly."

"What did you do after the delivery?"

"Well, I took you home. I couldn't believe I was leaving the hospital alone, carrying a newborn baby in my arms. Without Mum. My hands shook as I held you. I stopped myself from crying, this is exactly the role of a woman, to embrace a days-old child."

"Come on, Dad, you know that's not exactly true. Both the mother and the father should hug the baby."

"Son, I grew up in a different world. The infant's clinging to the mother's body was seen as the source of a proper development, the origin of an orderly world. People used to think that the first bonding of a mother and child was the source of all love and grace. I don't think so anymore, but before you were born I never ever considered the possibility that I would be the one to hold you close to my body, and not Mum. Fathers weren't even present at the birth, they waited outside the delivery room."

"So how did you manage when we went home?"

"How did I manage? God, I find it hard to think about it. When I bottle-fed you, you turned your head to my body looking for a breast. Sometimes you sucked my chest hair. But

I persisted, and fed you from a bottle. I got up at night, boiling water and mixing it with formula, waiting for you to satisfy your appetite, dozing while your body was resting on mine."

"And when Mum came home?"

"At first she sat next to me, watching me feed you. By then you were a couple of months old, looking from side to side, smiling once in a while. After a few days she decided she would feed you. You were crying out in hunger, so she picked you up, anxious and trembling, held you in her arms, and placed the bottle in your mouth. But you stopped crying, closed your lips tightly, and with eyes wide open looked at her with amazement. So you sat for a while, scrutinizing each other. Finally she looked down and said, 'He doesn't want me to feed him' and placed you in my arms, turning away and wiping her tears."

"Dad. Please stop crying. I'm so sorry. I didn't mean to remind you of all this."

"It's better this way."

"Are you okay?"

"Yes."

"Can I get you something to drink?"

"No, thanks, Amiri. I'll be fine in a minute."

"Are you sure?"

"Yes."

"Dad…"

"Yes, Amiri."

"I did something very wrong."

"I understand."

"I don't think you do."

"I think I do."

"I don't understand how it happened to me. I love Daphne, and I am so thrilled I will become a father."

"There is something very sensuous about impregnating a woman."

"Strange, but true."

"Amiri, I'm sure everything will be fine. Your birth was very unusual, and maternity wards are very different these days."

"Yes, I guess so. Oh, well, I'm going…"

"Where to?"

"Home. To Daphne."

Eighth Month

When I am sitting up straight at my desk you can see the movement within my protruding stomach, in spite of the wide shirt. A small bump, like a tiny hill, emerges on one side of the belly, disappears, and then resurfaces on the other side. Quick, delicate movements, something restless within the bubble, a body that seems to be trying to find its way out. I share a room with two colleagues, Gal and Rotem, devoted social workers. They giggle in a friendly manner every time they see that I'm watching my stomach intently. Gal, the mother of a three-year-old toddler, likes to tease me, "well, how many times did he move today? Were you counting?" She is such a good-hearted person, she never truly upsets me. Rotem, still single, looks at my stomach curiously and keeps asking me what it feels like, does his kicking hurt me, does he kick at night?

Today we open up early in the morning; before I was pregnant it was my favourite part of the day. I love to talk to people, to offer help, to suggest a solution no one had thought of. Gal, Rotem, and I became a special team: people come to the welfare office mostly looking for us. We listen attentively, ready to use any random or incidental piece of information to assist the needy. We are not like the "Aunties"—this is how we like to joke about the older social workers sitting in the next room, always dressed too elegantly, with fine jewellery and makeup, their hair perfectly coiffured, anxious that someone might mistake them for people asking for assistance. Gal likes to imitate them, exaggerating their apparent assumption that every person in despair needs to listen to a lecture: *why did you quit your job before you had another one? Why did you leave your husband? Is this a way to take care of a child?* She adopts a self-righteous expression, lifts her eyebrows and tightens her mouth, and Rotem and I burst into laughter. These performances, innocent and good-natured, asserted our distance from the "Aunties" and the different approach we adopted.

Ever since I became pregnant, and especially since my belly began growing, a certain laxity overtook me. The bubble is expanding and taking more space, not only in my body but also in my mind. When people walk in asking for help I try to absorb every word, but often during the conversation I find myself envisaging the hospital, recalling what the gynaecologist had said, or wondering why Amir disappears for so many hours. This morning Abraham, a man in his late fifties, came in, having recently been dismissed from a canning factory; unlike most unemployed men in his position, he keeps searching for work. He looks at me with dark eyes, his gaze vital and lively in spite of many disappointments, his grey hair curly, and his body muscular and sturdy. A man of his age has almost no chance of finding a job, and he knows that perfectly well—he wasn't even hired as a night guard. But he doesn't give up. His clothes are shabby yet he wears a freshly ironed white shirt, as if I am about to refer him to a job interview. Normally I look up the database—who knows, maybe I will find an employer looking for someone like him. But today I am impatient.

"I'm sorry, I already searched this morning, there's nothing new." Gal looks at me surprised, and Rotem immediately suggests she will search again. Abraham is encouraged, and moves to sit facing her. He places his hands on the desk, the huge, thick hands of a manual worker, full of small scars, remnants of years at the canning factory.

After he leaves a young girl walks in, chewing gum vigorously, heavily made up, dressed in black. Like her mother, she got pregnant by a boy, and now she wants us to help her get an abortion, "I don't want my mother's life, do you understand?" Here I am intrigued, the urge to comfort and help is reawakened, but her description of the pregnancy disrupts my thoughts: it is only the sixth week, there is no problem, she doesn't feel anything, only now did she realize she missed her period. The boy left as soon he heard she was pregnant, he doesn't even answer her calls, "So, I must have an abortion." Gal is looking at me, apparently seeing my gaze wandering around the room, passing over the young girl, who now becomes somewhat gloomy, and she hastens to offer help. The girl is annoyed, "Why can't only one of you help me?" Gal replies that she normally takes care of pregnancies and abortions and therefore she will assist her.

As she leaves Gal smiles at me, almost winking, and says, "I was also like that when I was pregnant. It's difficult to help others in these circumstances." She has a point; the pregnancy calls for an inner attention, concentrating on a process that will take place no matter what. For a moment I think it is a preparation, training the mother to detach from everything else and make room only for the child, but Gal continues, "I don't know why, I simply had no patience. I could hardly answer people who came in."

"Strange, I don't understand why," says Rotem. "Is it

because you are tired? Are you sleeping well?" she asks. Damn bird chirping, for a moment I think I can hear it, waking me every morning at five o'clock. I tell Rotem I am tired, but I don't think that it's the cause of my distraction. She insists: perhaps you need help? How will you manage when the baby is born? Will you return to work after maternity leave?

"I don't know. I want to return. I can't live without this place. And we need the money, our expenses will grow." Rotem keeps asking: how do other women manage? She turns to Gal, "What did you do, Gal? Return to work immediately?"

"I returned after six months."

"Did Jonathan have a nanny?"

"Yes. I found someone, though I paid her almost all my salary."

"So why did you return to work?"

"Because I had had enough of complete devotion to motherhood. It's an important stage in life, but it was over."

I can hear them talking, but something is blurring. The movements in my stomach increase, bringing stress, even fear: the creature living inside me is nervous and tense. Instead of listening to Gal, I think of Amir whispering in my ear last night, "Daphne, I am crazy about you," his body tucked in mine, the heavy belly moving slowly. If I could break out of myself I would give up these conversations altogether, leave the foetus here and go for a walk out in the battered streets of south Tel Aviv. The gentle rain would have comforted me, I would have skipped lightly over the puddles, as I used to do, wearing my blue jeans, simply wandering around carefree. Gal, always observant, watches me and asks: "Daphne, are you okay?"

"Yes, but I'm tired of this pregnancy."

"I know, the end is really hard."

"Not the end, all of it. I can't take it. I am terrified of the labour, I don't know how I will manage with a baby—maybe it is too early to have a child."

Rotem is horrified, but Gal smiles at me, her big eyes planted in a smooth face surrounded by golden curls, watching me with concentration. She then says, "Let me tell you, there is something you don't understand."

"I understand everything. I have heard, read, learned it all."

"You see everything but the main thing."

"What do you mean?"

"You don't understand what is means to be a mother. To be a parent."

"I understand. Soon I will have a child."

"Some things can only be comprehended through experience. You think you know what it will be like, but it is a transformation that can't take place before its time. When you get there you'll see that everything is different."

A sloppy old woman with a colourful headscarf stands at the door. Rotem and Gal are smiling at her kindly, asking if they can be of any help. She begins to complain: the welfare pension wasn't deposited on time, she finds it very hard, she has practically no money for food, a delay of a couple of days is disastrous, she doesn't understand what the problem is, on the second day of the month the money is always in her account, but now there seems to be a problem. Gal offers the woman a seat and turns to the computer, determined to find out why the pension was not deposited on time. And while she and Rotem are busy decoding the data, calling other offices and asking in insistent tones where the money is, I get up, put on my coat and leave the office, climbing down the dark stairway, pushing open the heavy metal door, and walking out of the building.

The man selling falafel next to the entrance is staring at the fine raindrops, holding a cup of steaming tea with mint. The smell of mint is so pleasant, fresh and slightly invigorating, I inhale it with pleasure and begin to walk down the street. Each step makes me realize how heavy my stomach is, its lower part almost rubbing against my legs. In spite of the houses revealing utter neglect, small dim shops with their sellers standing at the doorways awaiting customers, a shabby clothes shop called *The Palace Fashion*, there is something enjoyable about walking down the street. Trees are planted along the avenue and one can stroll slowly between them; their leaves drip tiny drops of water. The street benches are wet, so I keep walking. A handsome guy pulling a stubborn dog is walking towards me. Out of habit I lower my gaze, used to men scrutinizing me, but he passes without even glancing.

In three weeks' time I will no longer be coming here every morning. I will no longer drive from the northern part of Tel Aviv to the south. I will no longer observe, time and again, the transformation from streets lined by bright, tall buildings fringed with greenery to narrow alleyways so full of wintery puddles that I can hardly cross them.

I won't devote myself to helping those in need. I won't share a room with Rotem and Gal, struggling together with a bureaucracy entangled in its own rules, or laughing in good spirits. This thought brings tears to my eyes. Our office, so small that we could hardly squeeze three desks in it, became the most popular welfare office in Tel Aviv. Though there is hardly enough room to sit down, people wait patiently outside, sometimes for an hour or two, until we ask them in.

I see I have walked pretty far from the office, and decide to return. I see my reflection in the windows: a tall woman, with a pretty face, long red hair, wearing a grey sweater, stretching over her full breasts and huge belly, which looks almost impossible to carry. Will I return here after the birth? A sudden gust blows the dry leaves that have fallen from the trees up into the air; together they circle above the wet street and then descend, each to a different fate: one drops into a puddle next to the pavement, another falls on a bench, some blow down the street among the passers-by.

For a moment the sun breaks out from behind the clouds; a hint of great happiness is forming into an image of a baby I hold in my arms. His eyes are closed, his mouth round and sweet, his body-warmth blends with mine. I kiss his smooth moist cheek. My eyes are filled with tears. But then the sun hides and a dark cloud materializes in the distance, huge and lacking a distinct shape, approaching me slowly.

Even when my fear disappears, for fear is another creature that I carry within me, embracing the foetus kicking in my stomach, and I believe the delivery will go well, the future is still entangled and obscure. I push a stroller in which a plump baby is sleeping; Amir and I purchase a cradle, a chest of drawers, bottles, all shiny and beautiful; I return to work at the crowded welfare office; Amir returns home early, without calling to say he must finish something; I spot the glass cat, which I haven't been able to find since I became pregnant; I am thin again, the huge belly is gone; I put on jeans and a tight black shirt, black eye liner and shiny red lipstick; my mother tells all her friends that a charming new grandson has been born; I look for a nanny, but I can't find one I like; two o'clock in the morning, the baby is hungry and crying; Amir holds the baby, embarrassed, and says, "Daphne, take him"… It all circles and blends, and the future assumes an alarming shape.

I am back, standing next to the welfare building. Now the rain has stopped and many customers gather around the small falafel shop, each one asking for different toppings. The hands of the shop owner move so quickly as he prepares the food one can hardly follow them. I join the queue. The odours of deep fried food mix with the smell of mint—God, I am so hungry. I will take the falafel and drive home. I am eager to get into bed and close my eyes.

*

A calculation of future expenses adds up to a significant sum. I add a series of numbers, careful not to make a mistake: a cradle, a chest of drawers, a stroller, bottles, diapers, baby clothes. There is something annoying about checking the prices. Once in a while I omit one item, and then I add up the numbers again, getting a different total sum. Clearly both my parents and Daphne's will want to share some expenses, purchase a couple of things (it would be a mistake to deny them this pleasure), thus the calculation will probably change. Even though Daphne's mother has already pointed out that her older daughter has a used crib in perfect condition, and she could borrow a stroller from a friend, I fended off her resentment, I wanted everything to be new. The birth of our son will be a new beginning.

Today I gathered the courage to ask for a raise. Ever since I started working in this accounting firm I haven't set foot on the management floor. This morning I had an appointment with the boss, Mr. Schuster. His secretary asked me to wait for a couple of minutes until he would be free. Everything about this floor demonstrated wealth and success: a shiny burgundy wall-to-wall carpet, several orchids placed on a reception desk made of fine polished wood, a huge window on an upper floor with a full view of Tel Aviv (its older buildings, stretched to the horizon, appear to have no straight lines), several secretaries speaking in low voices on the phone, and a pleasant waterfall sculpture trickling down.

However, Mr. Schuster was the antithesis of his office's elegance. His suit, old fashioned and out of style, was a bit wrinkled, and he looked pretty tired, his eyes red and irritated. In an indifferent tone he inquired very simply as to why I had asked to meet with him. His manner left no room for what I had planned to say. Clearly he was expecting a quick, direct answer, so I said, "My wife is eight months pregnant. This is our first son. I would be grateful if I could have a raise."

Mr. Schuster looked at me straight in the face, but his blank expression did not reveal his thoughts. After a moment he said, "Well, I will look into it and let you know if it's possible." I mumbled my thanks on my way out and he waved his hand, perhaps greeting me, maybe saying goodbye, or simply suggesting that I get out of his office. The meeting lasted no more than a minute.

I returned to the junior accountants' floor and sat down by my desk, full of tidy piles of papers. There was no elegance here, only bare walls, computers everywhere, and endless papers with calculations of income and outgoing. I always place the receipts that clients send me in the metal tray on the left side, and after uploading the data to the computer, I move them to the right tray where they wait to be filed.

As I was sitting there, wondering why I hadn't explained my request in detail, the phone rang. Mr. Schuster's secretary wishes to let me know that he had authorized a five percent raise to my salary. Before I managed to reply, the call ended. There was no room for hearty thanks. Mr. Schuster had decided, I was informed, tomorrow human resources will be notified.

Still, I didn't want to be deprived of the joy from the good news, so I called Daphne. I heard the phone ringing, but no answer. When she is busy helping people she never answers the phone. Her devotion is endless. Even though she grew up in a pleasant neighbourhood in Tel Aviv, and her parents (though not wealthy) had always provided for her, she has always had a profound empathy for those in need. When we met, she told me that she was studying social work, and I thought it contained a seed of pretence, a need certain women have to appear kind-hearted and generous. But to my utter surprise I later found she had a subversive element, latent and invisible. Her empathy with the poor was always followed by an implicit accusation against a society that neglected them. Her huge eyes, encircled by dark shadows, concealed a deep scepticism in spite of their innocence. During her studies (she was an excellent student) she dismissed many theories on the sources of social disadvantage. Sometimes she even argued that these theories, if followed, would deepen the disadvantages of the poor. She even suggested they were aimed at self-justification. I was overwhelmed by her views. I never suspected Daphne could think this way, and I never thought people formulated theories merely to justify themselves. But I was completely enthralled by her rebellious spirit. With her gleaming eyes and shiny red hair, she explained that she would be a different kind of social worker, compassionate and without vanity. When she spoke like that, wavering between scepticism and enthusiasm, my indecisiveness suddenly disappeared and I kissed her for the first time, without hesitation.

After a couple of rings I knew she was busy and wouldn't answer the phone. I hung up and called my parents, eager to boast about my success, how I got a raise almost without any effort. I heard my father's soft voice. Even before he managed to say hello I told him about the appointment with Mr. Schuster. He kept saying "Well done, son" over and over again. I don't know why, but his desire to support me only made me resentful. Anyway the call was over quickly, and I was left sitting at my desk, staring at the phone, wondering with whom I could share the happy news.

As I was sitting there, reconstructing the very short meeting and the phone call that followed it, my gaze travelling round the walls of the office, lingering on the photos of my colleague's children, the phone rang again. Sari. I couldn't help the trembling that seized me, increasing with every ring, preventing me from taking the call or disconnecting it. Time and again she calls, she finds my determination for us to stop seeing each other amusing. Sometimes I think that if I had said nothing, she wouldn't have called. But my words, the attempt to break this carnal bond, to persuade myself that I can overcome lust, provoke her desire to see me surrender. And when I manage to avoid her calls she texts me,

"When will we meet?"

"Remember Wednesday morning?"

"I will be waiting for you tomorrow at one o'clock, at lunch break."

I ignore most messages, resolved not to give in, thinking of Daphne, of the baby about to be born. I even imagine what Mum would say if she knew. Despite all this, there are rare occasions where I meet her at her house. They could be counted on the fingers of one hand.

Strange, the excitement generated by this passion is never complete. I used to imagine this kind of lust as sweeping, intoxicating. Now I discover that it is blended with a touch of hatred; a loathing of both myself and Sari that never completely disappears. In every moment of pleasure there is a drop of anger, which I don't quite understand, a rage that increases gradually, nurturing the desire. Last time, standing at the door on my way out, I watched Sari lying naked on the bed (smiling without revealing her secret) and I felt that I detested her. The big breasts, the flat stomach, everything that seemed so seductive was now too full, almost disgusting. When I left I tried to smile and said: "You understand I can't go on like this?" and she (as always) looked at me with a hint of a smile, like a naughty, spoilt girl.

But most of the time, I don't answer her calls. There is no point in long explanations, everything is clear. The thought of Daphne finding out about us almost makes me faint. Every time I think about it I see her wide eyes looking at me with pain and accusation. Endlessly I imagine what would happen. I would deny it, say it isn't true; then I would start crying, ask for forgiveness, say I don't know what made me cheat on her like this, she knows how much I love her; I would beg for forgiveness, do anything to have her absolve me.

Sometimes I hope it would all be exposed, I prefer atonement to the fear.

Often after work I go to the coffee shop on Tel Baruch beach. In wintertime it is almost empty—the cold drives away even the regular customers. I sit at the bar on the deck, facing the sea, and once in a while I even walk down to the chairs on the sand, right next to the water. The dark sea is comforting. I watch the high waves, or I close my eyes and inhale the sea air. When will this baby finally be born?

It is so quiet and peaceful here at the office. There are two cases I need to finalize today. I turn to the computer, looking at long lines of numbers, all adding up "yearly expenses." I try to focus, but soon I realize that I can't, I'm too distracted. I decide to call Guy.

When I tell him how I got a raise he says, "nice, you nailed it!" chuckling and adding: "maybe I need a child too, so I can ask my boss for a raise." But when I add that the pay increase will begin one week before the baby's due date (which is next month), he answers coldly "Ah, I didn't know. Well, got to go, bye!" and hangs up.

I sit at the desk, still holding the phone next to my ear, wondering why Guy is so grumpy when I mention the coming birth.

Ninth Month

Winter makes every get-together more festive. The grey light makes lit rooms prettier, cold wind makes the heating cosier, wine and beer creates an even merrier atmosphere. Yet, I am eager to leave.

If I hear the word "pregnancy" one more time I will simply walk away. I can't take it anymore. Another discussion on the stages of giving birth, a detailed description on how the embryo turns in the womb, I have had enough of this. I will simply walk way, leave Guy delving into these stupid conversations, Daphne listening as if it wasn't her but another woman who was about to give birth, and Amir clinging to the pregnancy like a lifeline, so thin and serious, though sometimes he has this slightly sarcastic tone.

Especially now, as I am about to finish another renovation, this pregnancy is turning into such an undesirable unfolding. The owner waited for months for me to renovate the apartment on a high floor in the centre of Tel Aviv, overlooking the port. Friends told her that I "do a terrific job" and she was determined to have me change her home, giving it a modern, contemporary look. No matter what the cost is, she said, as long as you "turn it into an inviting, comfortable place". Sometimes I wonder why an interior decorator is needed in order to toss out unneeded stuff. People cling to old things—books that were gifts but no one has ever read them, dusty kitchenware placed in the back racks, old blankets that "it's a shame to throw out"—as if they held a potential for another life. When she first invited me to her apartment she pointed, with a mixture of pride and embarrassment, to an old mixer. "Can you believe it? I got it for my first wedding" she said, adding that she had never used it but "didn't have the heart to get rid of it". In spite of her generous smile she looked at me with some animosity; after all, she had hired me so that I would remove the old mixer, exempt her from the punishment of this gift, from the image of all the food she never cooked with it. A woman with a smooth face and grey hair, her mouth always covered with bright pink lipstick, she was determined to alter the apartment, to replace the heavy old furniture with light coloured sofas, to remove the old decorations and allow a new light to fill the place.

The second time we met, when I placed the plans for the renovation before her, she looked at me with mistrust. It was hard to imagine that the dark, respectable apartment could turn into a wide space completely filled with sunshine. The expensive old-fashioned carpets, faded over the years, created an impression that the air was filled with dust, even a hint of mildew, though the place was obviously very clean. A full, childish happiness fills me every time I put the drawings before a new client: the bewilderment, the scepticism, the hesitant questions. I reply with full confidence that the place would shed its old garments and adopt a clean, modern form. My ability to generate change fills me with pride. I answer every question patiently, elaborating on my choice of materials, on why a harmony of colour must be kept, although eventually a few contrasting splashes will be added, on why a wide open space should be maintained, though some corners are crucial for creating a lived-in cosiness, on why the bright Mediterranean light must penetrate but be toned down, to keep the place cool in the summer. Every choice I make is well reasoned: I will create a nearly perfect combination of grace and comfort.

But Rachel, my current client, was suspicious, and there was a sense of constant hesitation. Widowed in the Yom Kippur War, she remarried soon after to a wealthy lawyer. And though she immediately announced to me that money was not a problem, she would pay whatever it takes to make her home beautiful, she kept inquiring about the price of various materials—how much the Italian lights cost, is the fine leather furniture really that expensive, and so on. Her distrust revealed old anxiety: perhaps there would be a twist of fate again and a new unknown threat would emerge; perhaps there would be expenses that could not be met. But she quickly returned to, "as I have said, money is no problem".

The work had so far taken two and a half months and was about to be completed within a couple of days. Rachel insisted she needed to check how everything was coming along. Time and again she showed up without prior notice, taking the workers by surprise. "The inspector" they called her, since she had endless questions: why is a certain wood used in the kitchen and not another one, why is the paint on the walls different from the one in the catalogue, is the window frame installed properly, and so on. Unlike them, I enjoyed her questions. She was gradually absorbed by my profession, exploring the smallest details, listening attentively to long explanations. Until, finally, she looked at me almost with admiration, murmuring, "I knew what I was doing when I decided to wait for you. Everyone told me you were excellent."

She once wondered out loud if the work would be done on time. Unintentionally a condescending tone crept into my words—you know there are ten clients waiting for me, I want it to be ready on time as much as you do. Rachel smiled. My vanity seemed to support her good choice, and she said, "I always managed to find the best people in any profession."

When a project is finished I always insist that the client host a small event. No need to invite many people, just have a few friends over to toast to the new appearance. Family members are invited, perhaps some colleagues, Guy always comes along, proudly telling everyone he is my partner. The guests walk in with sceptical smiles, which then transform into forthright wonder: the tones match perfectly, the clean lines are pleasant, evoking functionality but not alienation, the plants are delicate, and the windows create the impression that they open onto an enchanted landscape. At once a couple of women ask for my card, declaring they also want to renovate their apartments. People walk around almost in awe, looking at me with astonishment, attempting to understand how such an inviting harmony was created, such a perfect integration between elements that seem so utterly different.

But this time, when we had returned home from a visit to Daphne and Amir, Guy said he wasn't sure he would be able to come to the event taking place in a couple of days as his boss asked him to finish some plans on a restoration of an old building in Tel Aviv. This was the first time he didn't sound eager to come, speaking with strange reserve, as if suddenly it was inappropriate to have these small parties I love to host. I gazed at him with surprise, without concealing my disappointment. He then said, "What does it matter, everyone there will adore you."

Apparently my face revealed my bewilderment since he

then added, "I promised Amir I would join him at the coffee shop on Tel Baruch beach."

"You would rather go out with Amir than come to my event?"

"Stop it, Abigail, it means nothing. I'll come next time."

"I can't believe it. I thought you rather liked these events."

"I come for you."

A thin, transparent thread, flexible and invisible, entangles us, slowly entrapping us, a gradually thickening yarn that could never be undone, its threads interlocking. Daphne's pregnancy is present here, existent, and can't be removed: the huge heavy stomach that she carries, and the infant that will spring out of it. Here no one is preparing a crib or a stroller, no one is purchasing bottles and diapers, there is neither excitement mixed with anger nor tense anticipation. In this home magazines cover the floor, wine and beer glasses are left on the tables, and jazz fills the air in the evening. We both sit at our drawing boards, thinking how to integrate a variety of details into one attractive shape. But lately Guy doesn't relax on the sofa, smiling, he doesn't pull me towards him saying, "for goodness sake, will you stop working..." The foetus kicking in Daphne's belly has moved in with us, disrupting our self-absorbed routine, one project after the other. It is following us everywhere: to decorated offices, fine restaurants, the gym, bars and parties; it simply won't leave us alone. I think we will never be able get rid of it.

"Guy, I told you. I don't want children."

"I know, but I thought you didn't really mean it."

"It's not for me."

"Tell me, does your mother know about this? Doesn't she care?"

"She knows. I think she understands. She found no

63

support in her family; it was mainly a burden. It was very hard to raise me alone. She doesn't want it to happen to me. I think what makes her truly happy is my professional success. I think she regrets not having chosen this path."

Guy listens attentively, his gaze fixed on me, seeking a hidden hesitation, some indication that a twist is about to take place. Something about his look brings up a childhood memory: I nap in bed, I open my eyes for a moment and see my father watching, alert. Small dark eyes set in a radiant, handsome face. When he sees I am awake a huge smile spreads on his face.

Guy lowers his gaze, and I see a tiny transparent tear rolling slowly down his tanned cheek. "Abigail, I think this isn't for me. I want us to have children. I know you told me, but I didn't think you actually meant it. I can't give up being a father." A muscular hand stretches towards me, softly caressing my hair and cheek, and then withdraws and disappears.

I go to the kitchen. The air in the room is stuffy, I need to open a window. Emptiness takes over me, a sort of deafness, a huge glass bell covers me and I can't hear a thing. Guy says something, his voice comes from the room but it can't penetrate the transparent sheet coating me. Guy wants children, he won't give it up. He loves me, but he wants to be a father. I sit down and put my head on the table, my forehead rubbing against the polished wood.

An old echo surfaces from an obscure place, syllables that hardly make words, a masculine voice and a feminine one blending into one another, creating a vague growl, "sweetie", "precious", soft words envelop me, a tune I think I have never heard. I try to listen to them but they echo within an inner space, in a hidden spot. A beautiful tenor singing a children's song, the word "hyacinth" is repeated time and again, utter pleasure fills me as I hear it, *daddy, keep singing*, someone lifts me and carries me to another place, another voice is coming from the background and then the voices disappear. My forehead aches. I lift my head and see Guy standing next to me. "Abigail, are you okay?" He is bending towards me, his golden curls shining and his eyes moist.

"Why is it so important to have children? Until Daphne became pregnant you never even thought about it."

"I don't know, I don't understand it myself. Suddenly it seems like giving up something really important. You know I didn't grow up in a stable family. I always thought it wasn't for me, that only people coming from a functioning family, with both parents present, want kids. I intended to invest all my efforts in my profession, and if I'm lucky I'll have a good partner—I did better than I expected here!—and life would be pleasant. I would have money and would live the good life. But Daphne's pregnancy made me realize that Amir will have something I will never have. I don't know how to describe it, but it's different from anything I have."

"So this is all the result competing with Amir? Unbelievable."

"I'm not going to pretend that it didn't start off as competition, but now it evolved into something else, unrelated to Amir. Maybe it is an innate human instinct, something beyond specific circumstances. I really don't know, a sort of desire to live on in my children."

"I don't get it, it feels like someone else is talking to me, not you. When did you ever care about being survived by your children? I have never heard you say anything about it before now. The Guy I know wants to plan amazing buildings, combine materials in a way no one thought possible, make a huge garden under a glass tent, construct with new materials—where did all this go?"

"It didn't go anywhere, it's still here. I still dream to fulfil all these plans. But there is also something else. Many creative people are parents, what has that got to do with it?"

"Ultimately every person has one main drive. If you want a family, you can't be devoted to work in the same way. I am not saying that no parents are professionally successful, but they have a different experience. They can't be creative in a complete way."

"Abigail, it's not a matter of choice. You might be right, but this is how I feel. Maybe right now it's not what you want but that might change. And you won't be doing it alone, if anything I'm willing to do most of the parenting work. There is nothing I want more than us having a child."

"It won't change, it won't change, how many times do I have to say this? It's not for me. I can't understand why you refuse to see this. And I don't understand what's gotten into you. And you better watch it, it's not that easy to fool around when you're a father…"

"What are you talking about? Who am I fooling around with? Are you saying I am cheating on you?"

"On me, no. But on others."

"What are you talking about?"

"I heard you cheated on all your girlfriends."

"How would you know?"

"I've heard. Everyone knows. Is this true?"

"They weren't my girlfriends. They were relationships that lasted too long, until they were over. I didn't really care about them."

"Oh, and what kind of father would you be?"

"What has that got to do with it? I am a different person with you."

"Come on, Guy, character doesn't change, and neither does family history."

"I don't want to have this conversation."

"I'm sure you don't!"

The slammed door echoes through the house. I drag my feet slowly and walk to the bedroom, collapsing across the bed. An unfamiliar exhaustion takes over. I close my eyes, repeating Guy's words time and again, trying to grasp every word, understand every sentence. My accusations were ludicrous, I am well aware of that, but the bitterness is rooting, spreading and expanding, making me angry again. I look up at the ceiling: the Japanese lamp is so beautiful, a delicate ink painting blended with calligraphy, made from of intricately designed folded paper, the lamp looks completely different at every angle, casting distinct shadows. As I am staring at the lamp an old childhood memory resurfaces:

When I was thirteen, my mum's sister came to visit us. She lived in New York, and came with her youngest son for a holiday. The encounter between them was odd, two women pretending that kinship necessarily creates intimacy. The polite kisses, the smiles, jokes about childhood friends, they all emphasized the alienation. Since then my aunt has never again come for another visit. Her son, then a chubby, little toddler, clung to his mother wherever she went. But after staying with us for a couple of days he became friendly with Mum and me. He brought lots of toys, and we observed him silently playing on the living room rug.

One evening Mum asked me to watch him, she and her sister were going out. "He is a quiet boy, no problem, he will have his dinner before we leave. You only need to watch him, play with him if he wants to, and around nine thirty or ten o'clock put him to sleep. He is very disciplined, he will do whatever you say." As they said goodbye, he looked sadly at his mother, but stayed sitting on the rug and playing. But after a couple of minutes I saw that he wasn't doing anything, and that tears were trickling their way down his cheeks, and he was wiping them with the sleeves of his pyjamas. I tried to cheer him up, persuade him that his mother would be home soon, suggested that we played together, but he looked at me with distrust and kept wiping his tears. Trying to distract him, I began to play with his Lego. I started fitting bricks of different colours and shapes, building things only to tear them down and start again on a new construction, I made a house, with a door, roof and four windows, then tore it down and made abstract shapes that came to form colourful patterns. Suddenly, I remembered that the toddler was there. I raised my eyes and saw that he had fallen asleep on the rug. I covered him with a blanket and carried on constructing various shapes in different colours.

The changing memory of the Legos is making me feel more energetic. For a moment I can actually recall the exact shapes and colours, and this creates a certain cheer. While thinking of colours I get up from the bed and tell myself it's about time to get ready for the event. I put on a black dress and high heeled shoes, cover my lips with shining red lipstick, splash on some perfume, and leave.

*

"Come on, Amir, it's so cold here. Are you sure you want to sit on the deck?"

"Yes. Look who's talking! Guy, you jog here at five o'clock in the morning…"

"But running keeps me warm. Never mind. Do you come here often?"

"Yes. I don't know, but somehow I find the rough sea relaxing."

"You've got a point. I like to run next to high waves. Let's have a beer."

"Sure."

"I wish I had my jacket."

"I left a sweater in the car. Would you like me to get it?"

"No, never mind. I'm fine."

"You look tired."

"I am exhausted. The restoration of the building on Shenkin Street is so complicated. We've kept the old structure, it's about a hundred years old, but we're constructing a new front. By the way, do you remember Michelle who went to school with us? An engineer who works with us knows her, and told me a shocking thing about her. She got married very young, she already has two children. A couple of months ago she found out that all these years her husband was also living with another woman, and they have a child. She told the engineer that she would see to it that her husband would never see their children."

"How did she find out?"

"I don't know. What difference does it make?'

"I don't know. It's interesting. Poor woman, but it's not fair that he won't get to see his children anymore."

"Not fair? Think what he did!"

"Of course, I'm not saying that what he did was acceptable. But why should the children suffer, not seeing their father?"

"Maybe it's better this way. He's hardly an ideal father, is he?"

"But people can find themselves in these circumstances. I daresay he's not proud of himself, but it can happen. Suppose he had an affair with this woman, she got pregnant and didn't want to have an abortion, what could he have done?"

"Come on, Amir, I can't believe you're saying this. People are responsible for their own lives."

"Only to a certain extent. You can't control everything."

"There are things that cannot be controlled, but this is not one of them! Living with two women and two families is choice, not destiny."

"True. Still, I feel sorry for him."

"I can't see why. I think it's despicable, dismissing the feelings of his family like that. My dad lives like that. He always cheated on my mum. As a child I saw him with his secretary, he used to wink at me, as though it was a mischievous prank. When I was older, about sixteen years old, I dared to ask him why he hurts Mum like that. Do you know what his answer was? 'It's who I am.' I try not to think about it because I am always so overwhelmed with anger. 'That's who I am!' Nothing touches him, not my mum's tears, not my anger, not even the threatening phone calls from the women he deserted. 'That's who I am,' that's all."

"I'm really not defending him. I'm sure he hurt you and your mother, but maybe there are some things that he can't control, at least not entirely."

"No. What appears to be giving in to lust is really a determined resolution: fully pleasing yourself and ignoring others. In fact, it's control over your life, and not the other way around."

"Come on, Guy, are you saying that we don't have weaknesses, desires that are stronger than us?"

"Don't you think my dad could have acted in a different manner? He didn't even bother to conceal his affairs. In fact, I think he rather wanted me to know about them. His world is simple, divided into men and women; all other things are negligible, even fatherhood. A sort of belief that the only truth—and the deepest—is the attraction between the sexes, and renouncing it is denying the obvious. If you think this way, there isn't much room for paternal feelings."

"Do you think men are not attracted to women anymore when they become parents? It is almost like saying they aren't human."

"I can't understand why you insist on siding with him. I'm talking about accepting responsibility for your actions, not your thoughts. Don't you think people behave differently when they become parents? I think it's a consequence of a fundamental human need to protect one's children. This is exactly what my dad is lacking. He doesn't even understand why I don't live the way he does."

"Listen, Guy, something ends when you become a father. In spite of the happiness, there is also a loss; dreams about certain adventures simply crumble and fall apart. It's very likely they would never have been fulfilled, but it makes no difference. The closer it gets to the birth, the delivery, the more real and vital the very long trip becomes—the one I'll never take. I add more and more details: places, foreign languages, women. I can even feel the homesickness that is part of it. But once I have given it up... well, some resentment inevitably mingles with my immense happiness."

"But that's true for any choice you make. If you choose one thing, you lose something else. It's always like that. I really love my work, but in the past I thought of becoming an engineer. When I decided to be an architect I also made another choice: not to be an engineer."

"Yes, but in principle you could stop working as an architect and turn to engineering. I know it's not going to happen, but knowing that it is possible makes the choice easier. But having a child is altogether different. It's something you can never ever undo. There is no way to retract the decision to bring a child into the world. You do something that will always shape your life. And in spite of the happiness, it's also difficult."

"Well—"

"It also changes your relationship as a couple. As much as you may love your wife or girlfriend, the possibility of breaking up is always there. But having a child together changes the nature of that connection. I feel this very clearly about Daphne. Of course I want to be with her, and we have been married for a couple of years now, but since she became pregnant something has changed. From now on there is an unbreakable tie between us. Having a child really does change everything. I'm very glad we are going to have a baby, but it's also a bit oppressive."

"Come on, Amir, people divorce, today more than ever. Parents who don't want to live together split up."

"Of course, I'm not saying it isn't possible. But the connection with the mother of your children will always be there, even if you don't see each other. Needless to say I don't want to separate from Daphne, but now I know that even if I wanted to, it would be impossible."

"Interesting. I feel I choose to live with Abigail every single day. On the one hand, it's very gratifying, it means I live like I want to, with the woman I love. On the other hand, it's also a bit oppressive. There is something pleasant about life simply happening, without having to constantly make a decision. In a way, a couple becoming a family is the natural thing, as if this is how it is supposed to be."

"I don't know what 'natural' is – we are so remote from

nature that it's almost meaningless. I wish I knew what is the 'right' way to live."

"Frankly, it seems to me that what you are saying is true on a theoretical level, but not connected to everyday life. Future fatherhood seems to make you very happy, but it is also stressful. It is something completely new, which you have never experienced, so you're stressed. The point is not the relationship with your partner, but fear of what the future holds. Your life is about to change dramatically, and you're not sure in what way, and it's hard."

"You admit that you choose to be with Abigail every day. So the theoretical issue is there, isn't it? Well, it's true for me as well."

"Could be. Maybe. I don't really get what you're saying. Are your parents excited about the baby?"

"Yes, but it's not all happiness. Remember I told you about my own birth? It was traumatic for them. And now it resurfaced again, especially for Mum. Ever since Daphne became pregnant she is constantly tense and worried, full of anxiety as the labour approaches. You wouldn't believe where she went yesterday."

"Where?"

"To the synagogue."

A Day before the Delivery

How did I end up here, on the edge of being a grandmother? I am still not sure… The wooden decorations on the walls, the creaky benches, the prayer books piled up on a table, the Torah arc closed, and the cantor casually walking around the synagogue… A strange and alien spirit fills the place. I came here gasping, I thought I would faint. A terrible anxiety took over me, and my trembling knees almost made me trip and fall.

It all started when I went to the greengrocers. A nice shop with excellent produce, I love to go there in the morning and get vegetables for dinner. The owners, a father and son, Arabs from the Galilee, greet every customer in an effusive manner, asking repeatedly how they are doing today. The father, a man about seventy years old, smiles at the customers but grumbles quietly if someone complains about a high price. The son keeps saying "no problem" almost as though it was a greeting. As I entered the shop this morning the father smiled at me and said, "I understand your daughter-in-law will give birth any minute now. I hope all goes well."

Strange, but something about these innocent words suddenly revived the memory of Amir's birth… In an instant the spirit of Jerusalem materialized in the small shop, I am not sure why; perhaps the fruit stalls, or the scent of a food market that fills the place, the mixture of Hebrew and Arabic the father and son were speaking, or "I hope all goes well"— our neighbour in Jerusalem used to say that before Amir was born. Sharp pain, a whip hit me, a sort of painful contraction that left me pale and breathless. I thought that in a moment I would collapse on the floor, giving birth. The father looked at me, bewildered, and said: "Are you okay?" I muttered that I'll be back in a minute, and walked outside.

Haggard breathing that almost didn't allow any fresh air to enter the lungs, my temples throbbing, pain ebbing and flowing, agony and relief, will overwhelm Daphne, her body will convulse, her long hair will be covered with sweat, cries of pain will fill the room, Amir will be weeping, he won't be able to take it, wishing to help but unable to do so. The foetus is too big, his head will be too big to pass through such a narrow passage, he will be ready to be spewed out into the world yet unable to squeeze out of Daphne's body, which must tear for him to be ejected. He will be caught there for hours, between womb and life, unable to resume a foetal position but incapable of stretching his limbs, his life will depend on the umbilical cord that would gradually wrap around his neck, who knows how long he can survive like that, he may suffocate any minute. I couldn't breathe, I needed some fresh air, I needed some fresh air.

I was walking like this in the street, shivering and breathless, struggling to ward off this imaginary birth which went so wrong, but in vain... An intense fear, its roots so deep they cannot be comprehended, grasped me. A neighbour who passed by greeted me, but I couldn't reply. All I could see were pavements, sky and blazing sun. As I was walking I happened to notice that the doors of the Ashkenazi Orthodox synagogue were open. My feet carried me inside. The hallway was cool and pleasant, yet it still somehow reminded me of an apartment building's stairway. A short dark man in Jewish Orthodox dress appeared from a side door. He smiled and said, "Hello. I am the cantor. Welcome." and disappeared. I climbed the stairs to the women's section and sat down. One elderly lady sat alone in the corner of the front bench, turning the pages of her prayer book and murmuring prayers.

Something about this place brought me relief... Only rarely do I go to a synagogue, and when I do, I always try to leave as soon as I can. But this time I sat there, looking around, and slowly the anxiety began to dissipate. I am not sure why... but I found the lack of magnificence consoling. Dust between the benches, some prayer books with pages slightly torn, the wooden decorations on the walls a bit chipped, a sweater someone had left on a seat, they created a certain scepticism, removed the need for tears and fervent prayer. I admit that there was something awe-inspiring about the Torah arc, its heavy curtain moved slightly as a sudden gust of breeze fills the place, turning the pages of the prayer book in front of me, but the cantor quickly closed the window with a creak. The old woman in the corner turned her gaze from the book to me, still murmuring prayers. Bewilderment filled her face as she observed me wiping a tear. Enough, I don't need to be here anymore. I am calm now, the fear has dissipated, and anyway, there is no room here for my oaths and vows.

*

"What were you doing there? I don't understand."

"I told you, I wasn't feeling well, so I went in to sit down for a while."

"You could have sat down elsewhere. Why there, of all places? I don't like that place."

"Neither do I, really, I just had to rest for a while."

"Was there anyone there?"

"The cantor, and an old woman, praying. I don't understand why it bothers you so much."

"I don't like synagogues. There is something so mundane about them."

"Mundane?"

"Yes."

"Why?"

"I don't know. They don't create awe."

"I don't understand, why does is bother you if people want to pray?"

"I have no problem with a person praying by himself. But I don't like this institution where everyone prays together."

"Maybe it's easier than praying alone."

"Maybe. I don't know. I don't like it."

"Eventually we all pray, even secular people. When it comes to giving birth, sickness, death, people turn to prayer. Even non-believers."

"You mean that when there's nothing left to do, people pray?"

"It's admitting that there are things beyond your control."

"Come on, Rebecca, I have no doubt there are many things beyond my control. But I don't think that prayer will make a difference. I try to see that the doctors are accomplished, the hospital has a good reputation, that they don't act irresponsibly."

"But sometimes nothing helps... You know that there are times when even the best doctors can't help."

"So what good would prayer do?"

"Listen, Aaron, prayer is part of being human. People always prayed, it's like singing, dancing, drawing. It's simply part of us, and it makes no difference whether we are religious or secular."

"Well, never mind. I'm glad you feel better."

"I had a terrible anxiety attack, I could hardly walk, and simply found myself there."

"I understand, but—"

"I honestly didn't go there to pray. But when I was there… I sat in the women's section, the old lady in the corner murmured her prayers, the cover of the Torah arc slightly moved, I overheard the cantor speaking in the entrance hall, he kept saying 'God willing'—and suddenly a prayer broke out, a sort of whimpering, a begging. At that moment I was willing to make any concession, to take any vow so that her labour would go well. Don't look at me like that, mocking me."

"Mocking? Not at all."

"I am ashamed of this prayer. It is so childish."

"I don't think that prayers are heard. But there is only one prayer I find worthy—childlike, innocent, full of tears and cries, lacking hesitations or calculations. *Please God. Please. Please help me.*"

Five Hours before the Delivery

The scent of rain is coming from the yard. In spite of the chill I sit in the old armchair on the porch, inhaling the clean air with pleasure. I lean back, almost unable to carry the huge bubble my body is wrapped around; I am covered with a duvet, my swollen feet propped up on a footstool Amir brought me. My head against the headrest, I am looking at the sky brimming with clouds and water drops. The tall trees surrounding the porch gently bend their tops, stretching wet branches to the soaked ground. Strange chirping comes from the grass, for a moment I think I see an animal running across the yard, and sad barking is coming from a nearby house. If you look at the trees around the porch at night you can almost imagine that the house is deep in the woods, and that I am a little girl who has lost her way.

I think that if I close my eyes the strange contractions the bubble is making will vanish. In the last couple of hours it began to shrink into itself, moving slightly from side to side; detached from its position it began to sail slowly toward the birth canal. An enormous bubble, expanded so much within my body that I can't carry it anymore, and now it's unhurriedly making its way out.

Sitting here beneath the trees observing the contractions,

a paralyzing fear drives away the indifference and despair of the last days. According to the doctor's calculation, I was supposed to have given birth two weeks ago. The forty-week calendar terminated fourteen days ago, and since then a different counting was taking place, with a new rhythm. Gone is the growing tension as the due date approached; now time passes slowly, almost unnoticed. From early morning hours, as the weight of the bubble wakes me, through the slow drive to the social welfare office, where everyone is begging me not to come to work—I am about to give birth any minute now, how will I manage to get to the hospital quickly? But I insist and come to work, though now I need the lift to get to the office on the first floor. People who walk in immediately turn to Gal and Rotem, as though it is obvious a woman in my condition can't be very helpful. I see them avoiding my desk, but I am too distracted to be insulted. I walk slowly to the fridge, fill a cup with cold water, and then walk back to my desk, sitting carefully, calculating how to tilt the extra weight I carry without tripping and falling.

When I return home I try to do some housework. Anything that can stop me from thinking about the labour is welcome. Strange that in the first months I found it hard to admit that a living creature was growing within me, whereas now the thought that my body once existed without the foetus now seems bizarre. I got so used to this duplication, a body within a body, foetus within mother, that I now find it almost impossible to believe that my body will soon contain only itself. The huge stomach, the heavy breasts, the plump face and arms, it all seems so irreversible.

Yet staring into the hallway mirror, I cannot recognize myself. An alien woman gazes back at me. Despite the cold of winter, her face is covered with a sheen of sweat, her hair hangs lifelessly and there is no trace of the former fragility of her body; it now has a singular purpose, a determined utility.

My mother keeps telling me how she gained so much weight when she was pregnant, and how her body never regained its former shape. "You'll see, you'll be very tired, it's not that simple," she says, suggesting that all women suffer a single fate that must be accepted. Sometimes I think she looks at my growing body with some delight. Here, now you will finally understand that mothers end up heavy and thick, and any attempt to deny this is pure vanity. She often visits us, walking between the rooms as if she has to check whether the house is ready for a baby, peeking into wardrobes, moving kitchenware from one place to another. Every time I try to say something about the fear of the birth itself she leaps into long descriptions of other births: how I came into the world, how my sister gave birth, she even talks about her own mother. And so the delivery turns into a mass event, shared by countless other women, and the minor details are absorbed into a general suffering that has always existed. Once she even elaborated on how our cat gave birth, mewing in pain all night, Mum thought she was dying, but in the morning she found five cute kittens suckling, and the cat exhausted. And so the coming of a living creature into the world becomes an event shared by all mammals, and there is no room for the fear spreading within me, spreading like the bubble itself.

Amir offers to help time and again, explaining that I need to avoid any stress. But beyond his kindness I can see a terrified look. He observes my body secretly, thinking that I can't see him, and his countenance reveals something reminiscent of hate. As if some cruel fate has forced on him a woman whose body is constantly expanding, and there is no way to stop this swelling of the flesh. He often talks about how happy he is about becoming a father, but his eyes betray a tortured resentment. He places a soft cushion behind my head so I will be comfortable, but his voice seems to hesitate. He buys my favourite chocolates, but before he hands them to me he peeks at my huge belly. When we walk in the street he smiles at me, but his eyes follow other women.

Yesterday at noon only Gal and I were in the office. We are normally very busy at lunchtime but now an unusual silence filled the place. It was raining heavily, and then it started to hail, hard little balls bouncing from side to side, covering the gloomy street with a veil of white. A gust of wind pushed a shutter loose, which hit the external wall of the building over and over again. It appeared as though everyone was waiting for the storm to abate. I had some cold water, Gal made a cup of coffee. Watching the storm together, listening to the whistle of the wind, Gal said, "Daphne, you look so sad. Don't worry, the pregnancy will be over soon and everything will be okay." I looked into her blue eyes that now were extremely serious. She gazed at me intently, waiting patiently for me to say something. I simply stared at the wall. Silence fell in the room. Gal said nothing. I got up, returned a couple of files to the cabinet, threw some papers into the trash and moved the mail to the outbox beside the door. Gal still said nothing, only looked at me, waiting. Finally I said quietly, "You know, there's something really distorted about the fact that I am pregnant." She opened her eyes wide, and again said nothing. "I mean that I am pregnant and Amir stays unchanged. I know it sounds really silly, but I am fat and heavy, and he's the same. We were always equals, and now, suddenly, I am the only one who is changing."

"You do know that you're talking to a single mum, don't you?"

Gal had never before elaborated on why she had chosen to have a child without a husband or partner. Though she had told us about her life before she came to Tel Aviv, she had said nothing about being a single mother. She had grown up on a farm in the north, but had felt that there was something limiting about life there and so had decided to leave. Still, something about her countenance suggested that she had lived in the country for years, and was not originally from a city. Big, blue eyes and curly hair, she had a freshness that women more beautiful than she lacked. She moved to Tel Aviv and got a job as a waitress because she was saving money for a trip abroad. After a couple of months, she left for India, hoping to explore nearby countries. But after a month her friends were surprised to find that she had returned. When they asked worriedly if anything was wrong she said simply: no, I just realized this is not what I was looking for. The horrible poverty that I have seen has made me understand that what I really want to do is help people, nothing more.

After she finished her studies and became a social worker, she got a job at the social welfare office in Jerusalem. Surprisingly, she was involved in many arguments, in spite of her easy-going nature. She told Rotem and me that she couldn't cope with the condescending attitude of the social workers, and how they often treated people in an imperious manner simply because they could. She was once at a meeting in which the other social workers dispassionately agreed on a child being taken from her home. When she commented on their detached attitude they looked at her with contempt and wondered aloud if she had chosen the right profession.

Eventually, she came to the welfare office in Tel Aviv. The "Aunties" examined her from head to toe, inspecting the somewhat sloppy clothes and the wild curly hair. They then suggested that she sit in the next room. They failed to see that this insulting suggestion would dramatically change the office. Gal cleaned the small room, transforming it from a cold place into a pleasant, inviting office, and began to assist people with enthusiasm and devotion. Within a month it became the favourite place for people coming to the office. Everyone knew that "the blonde social worker" did whatever she could to help, without demanding an explanation on why life had gone so wrong. The long line outside the door with a small welcome sign caused the Aunties no end of envy and agitation. They couldn't persuade even one person in the line to switch to their office, though they promised that they would be far more helpful. Everyone looked at them without saying a word.

When Rotem and I began to work there, Gal gladly made room for us, feeling we shared her good spirit. She knew how to extract information from severe-looking clerks; persuade doctors to accept urgent cases; fend off exasperated teachers; and we gladly took her advice. She introduced herself as "a social worker and Aviv's mother" without mentioning any man, making her single motherhood clear. Her desk was full of photos of Aviv: in the pool, at nursery school, with Gal, with Grandma and Grandpa.

But yesterday, when we were alone together in the office, she said for the first time "single mum." I lifted my eyes from the table and stared at her. Embarrassment blended into my misery, but Gal immediately said, "Don't worry, I'm okay talking about it. Why do you think it is unfair that you are pregnant?"

"I know it sounds silly, but it breaks an equilibrium that was always there."

"What do you mean?"

"You know, in any relationship there is always an implied threat. Something that is never said but is still there, even when a couple is in love. Each one can betray the other, find another partner. Normally people don't carry out the threat, but it creates a certain equilibrium. Yet it's shattered during pregnancy."

"Yes, I know. The truth is I never wanted to live within this equilibrium. It's not for me, this threat. It is against my character."

"What do you mean?"

"Exactly what you said. Every time I had a boyfriend I could feel this threat, and I didn't want to live like that. But I really wanted to be a mother, so I decided to have a child alone, without a partner. I won't tell you it's easy, it took my parents ages to get used to it, but for me it was the only option."

A huge bolt of lightning flashed across the sky, a violent thread of light, and then a horrible peal of thunder was heard, rattling the building. The rain was pelting down, and a couple of drops crept through an invisible crack in the window. Water fell from the sky and flooded the street. Gal's eyes were shining as she looked outside. We both stood by the window, looking at the rain, as she said, "It wasn't like that for my parents, I'm sure. A man and a woman who were unconditionally devoted to each other, without threats or conditions. The possibility that either one would leave simply didn't exist. I'm not sure it was love; perhaps a clear acceptance of them being married forever. Nowadays there's no such thing." As I turned my head and looked at her, I saw that she was wiping away the tears that were streaming down her face and dripping onto her shirt.

The bubble contracts again, shrinking into itself. Amir is glancing at me from across the room, asking me how I am feeling. When I tell him that the contractions have begun but that it is too soon to go to the hospital, his eyes sparkle. Night birds spring up with a cry, a bending branch is moaning, the wind is weeping, and a roaring thunderclap is heard from afar. The fear, which I always knew existed, turns into a petrifying horror. The understanding that a living creature is about to tear his way out of my body nearly makes me faint.

*

When the phone rang I answered it quickly. The thought of Daphne finding out that Sari is calling scares me to death. I place the cell phone right next to me (casually), and try (unsuccessfully) to wait two rings. I take the call at once (trying to create an impression that there's no rush). Even though I asked Sari to be careful not to call me in the evening, I'm afraid she will surprise me—she burst into laughter and said, "I'll try, but I am not sure I can manage this." Knowing that someone is trying to ruin my life makes me furious. But then I remember that this is all my fault, and a gloom overwhelms me. Even if Sari did call, I'm not sure that Daphne would notice. She seems so detached, immersed in her pregnancy and ignoring everything else. Yesterday I suggested we go out to the local coffee shop, but she dismissed it saying that she was too tired and can hardly walk.

A withheld number. A familiar, feminine voice comes from the other end. "Amir, what's up?" Heddy, my colleague. I sigh with relief, but then I panic, (realizing that I sighed out loud). "What's up? What's going on with Daphne?"

"Nothing really. We're waiting. It's been two weeks since the due date. I don't know what will happen, I guess at a certain point she'll be admitted to the hospital."

"Listen, I really do understand, but you have to come to

work. These last two days you've gone home early, leaving me with loads of work. We need to finish the annual statement by the end of the week, and I won't be able to do it by myself."

"You're not serious, are you? My wife is about to give birth any minute now. I have to be around to help her."

"I really understand, but I won't be able to finish the work without you, and Schuster will be so mad if it isn't ready."

"Listen, will you do me a favour, and for once do my part? I'll make it up to you, I promise."

"It's not a matter of principle, I'd be happy to do your part, but I need to pick up my kids from nursery school. My husband works nights, and there is no one to help me with the boys. I really have to go."

"Heddy, I can't leave Daphne by herself."

"I know, but I can't leave the boys by themselves either."

When I told Daphne I needed go to the office for two hours she opened her huge eyes and looked at me sadly (for a second I thought I saw tears in her eyes, but apparently I was wrong). She asked why, and when I explained she said it's okay, if the contractions start she would call me, I could get home in about twenty minutes. Her understanding that I had to go brought me to tears. Over and over again, I asked if she could manage by herself and promised that if the contractions started in earnest, I would be back immediately. I then made her a light dinner and brought her a warm duvet because she wanted to sit on the porch in spite of the cold. I placed the phone right next to her (just in case) and gave her a bottle of cold water.

The streets are flooded. Water spurts from the car wheels. I am driving rapidly to the tower in the centre of the city. I brake hard at the traffic lights, overtake cars carelessly, splashing water on the passers-by until finally screeching to a halt in the car park. Some people are still working at this hour (though in most offices the lights are out). I open the door, switch on the light, sit by my desk, and turn to the computer to see what has been done so far.

A long column of numbers breaks down and rearranges itself in a new order, adjusting to the different patterns: revenue, inventory, cash flow, equity, a multitude of items, each swallowing endless digits. You have to read every line, look at every number, check in case a mistake, or even fraud, is concealed somewhere. Line after line, concentration is required here, slow and systematic, avoiding confusion, following the inner logic of the digits and checking if they add up to a reasonable amount.

Fifty items need auditing. I did seven, another one, another one, what time is it? Nine thirty-six. The phone isn't ringing, Daphne hasn't called (and neither has Sari), apparently no contractions yet. Maybe I should call her? Better not, she might be asleep. Well, I'm thirsty.

I made myself a coffee and carried on working. Two more items done. One was unbelievably long, endless sub-items within sub-items. Here, the inventory is audited. I forced myself to check over the statement, anything to avoid Mr. Schuster's anger, I will work all night and finish the whole thing. What time is it? Eleven minutes past ten. Daphne hasn't phoned (apparently the labour won't happen tonight). What time— Twelve minutes past ten. Another item. Cash flow. That's an easy one. I burrowed into the numbers, trying to examine every single one, but fear of the coming birth turned all those items into cries of pain I thought that I could already hear. What time? Ten twenty. Daphne still hasn't called.

I forced myself to keep on working and I managed to look into eight more items. But by then I was exhausted. I was tired of this rigorous review of numbers, and the approaching birth was gradually forming in my mind. What do I care? I will tell Mr. Schuster that I audited everything. Anyway he can't tell (he never actually supervises the work), all he cares about is letting the client know that the statement is ready and charging the fee. No one will know that I never examined it. Suppose it has some mistakes, and maybe even fraud—what does it matter? At most, the firm will make more money and conceal revenue from the IRS. What has that got to do with me? The chance of getting caught is practically negligible.

I skimmed the entire annual statement, as though a hidden eye was watching me and I had to prove that I have actually examined the numbers (maybe I was creating a seed of self-justification, in case I would be asked whether I thoroughly audited the entire statement or not). After a couple of minutes I left a note on my colleague's desk: "Heddy, I've worked until late at night and managed to do most of it. Eight items need auditing. Please do that, and we will have the statement ready by the end of the week."

The falling rain comforted me on the drive home. It seemed as though the water spattering over the car was washing away my sins. An invisible hand, ancient and obscure, was preparing me for the birth of my son. Daphne sat on the porch, exactly as I had left her, "I'm having contractions, but I think it's still too soon to go to the hospital," she said.

Delivery

A wide strap is tightening around my entire lower torso, rubbing against my belly, indifferent to the pain it causes. A hidden pressure is created, its source unknown, and it seems that in a moment the strap might unfasten and the body would have some relief. But the pressure increases, the strap tightens even more, encircling the huge bubble, threatening to split it and crush the foetus inside. I am out of breath; I may choke any minute, when will this horrible strap stop gripping and squeezing me, as if I weren't carrying a child. But I can still stifle the cries of pain, surely this will all be over in a minute. I will take a deep breath, think about something else, close my eyes, when will this torture end, I can't take it anymore, when will it be over

"Too late for an epidural. You're fully dilated. Inhale some gas, and then take a deep breath. When the contraction is over, try to rest."

Huge burning iron shears gradually take hold of the big bubble, their blades clutch me, splitting my body, tearing away the foetus. Thousands of capillaries attaching it to me are ripped in an instant, scorched by the hot blades; blood covers the bubble, pulled down by an irrepressible force. The body is torn apart, the blood vessels are utterly destroyed—

—a pain that I had never before known, eradicates any feeling, silences any thought, removes any embarrassment. A painful shriek breaks out, spreading through the room. Amir's hand holds me even tighter, as his other hand wipes away the tears. I am afraid that he will faint, right next to the delivery bed.

"Don't hold your breath, keep breathing, inhale some gas and relax. For the next contraction, try to push harder."

Barbed wire surrounds the bubble, as if someone had tied a strand around it in order to pull it out. The sharp ends scratch me as they pull the bubble downwards. My body is swathed in sweat, it is pouring down my hair, breasts, abdomen, a foul sour odour fills the room, vile and sickening. My body exudes a repulsive turbid liquid that spills on the floor and is repeatedly mopped up. I wish the bubble would come out, I am trying as hard as I can to push it out but I fail, it is too big, it is tearing my body and it won't come out.

"Here, I'll wipe your face. Don't worry, we'll clean you up immediately after the delivery."

Though I hear the cries of pain, I can barely feel that it is me who is howling. The burning iron shears grab the bubble and pull it in a circular motion.

"The head is there, try to push harder!"

—as if it were within my power to prise apart these iron fingers. My legs are spread, my body is sweating, my pale and lifeless skin makes me sick, my nipples seem very dark, almost black, my knees are rough, my feet are distorted, and then an inner rupture makes an inhuman cry come out of my mouth.

"The head is out, another little push."

I am exhausted, the room is spinning, I am falling into an abyss, leaving my torn body on the delivery bed, I am detached from it, withdrawn. The doctor bends forward and with a swift motion pulls out

"Here we go, we'll turn him upside down and he'll start to cry. Hear that? What a beautiful baby. Mazel Tov, mum, you have a son, congratulations. Yes, everything seems fine, we'll have him cleaned in a minute. Would you like to hold him first? Here you go. Just a minute, I need to see that the remaining placenta is removed from the uterus. Excellent. Dad, do you want to cut the umbilical cord? No problem. How are you feeling? We'll take the baby away for a couple of minutes, transfer you to another room, and then have him brought to you."

*

Panic. Terrible panic. Horror that I might be sucked into some dark, obscure place, humid and steamy, like a well. A smell foul and distressing, yet achingly familiar, fills the place.

Crying. Screaming.

Long red hair, soaked with sweat, twisted and entangled, lies on ivory breasts. A pale abdomen, shuddering and quivering, shrinking and stretching, gradually gaping, ripped and bleeding. The legs wide open, placed on the foot supports, thin and lifeless, resembling crutches that would never be able to gracefully hold her body again.

A body unable to expel another body from within itself.

The doctor and the midwife exchange incomprehensible words, syllables only they can understand. They talk to Daphne in gentle soft tones, as though she were a sweet girl who has fallen and injured her leg, and now the wound must be disinfected and covered with a clean bandage—in spite of her shrill cries spreading through the room, filling every corner (she is like an animal caught in a trap and unable to escape, groaning with fear and pain). When she stops for a moment she looks at me surprised, as if she had just found out that I am here. Dizziness, the room is spinning, Daphne's face seems vague, slightly blurring the impression of her pain, I must take a seat.

Anger fills me as I suddenly realize that against my will I am thinking of Sari lying naked on her bed, her gaze seductive and her smile distant. Sari blends into Daphne, together they become a single woman, crying and laughing, slender-figured and full-figured, sad and giggling, giving birth and enticing: I am not sure whether I should stretch out my arms to her or flee, but I am terrified. I must drive Sari out of here, I don't know how she stole into this room (full of sultry steam), provoking a hatred that I didn't know I was capable of. For a moment I feel that if she had actually been in the room, I could have hurt her, grabbed her by the hair and yanked her out into the corridor.

Instinctively I get up and resume my place next to Daphne, who is whimpering and crying, moaning and screaming in pain. I take her hand, muttering strange instructions, "take a deep breath" that I don't understand, lost, waiting for the baby to rip her body and come into this world. I can't take her pain any more, my sweetheart, the tears running down her face, her fingernails stabbing my hand.

The room is filled with a foul smell, a strong light is illuminating Daphne's ravaged body, the sound of the baby's heartbeats plays over the monitor, blood spills on the floor, the doctor and midwife exchange words while giving Daphne instructions. She is stretched on a strange bed, half sitting half lying, stained towels piling up around her, obscure medical tools have been placed besides the doctor, all sorts of machines surround me. This place is unbearable.

I can't take it anymore: the pain, my sweetheart's pain, the tears sliding down her face, her nails digging into my palm. Daphne, my love, my precious, it will be over shortly, the suffering will end and our son will be born, only I don't know if I can stand another minute.

Two Hours after the Delivery

A tiny head, covered with a pale blue hat, is resting on my collarbone, seeking refuge from light, unfamiliar air; there is the sweet, warm smell of a body only just emerged into the world, eyes closed, a rounded, slightly protruding mouth, thin eyebrows, his skin peeling a bit. I hold him, breathing in the scent, such a pleasant, milky fragrance, flesh without the slightest trace of sweat or dirt. I caress his cheek anxiously, my finger looks huge next to the tiny cheek, it seems that one careless move might hurt my son. Yes, this is my son. I am a mother and I have a son. I keep repeating these words, closing my eyes, stifling laughter that may burst out any moment into a roar of pure happiness.

Again I touch the soft cheek with my finger, careful not to pull at the tiny pieces of skin, two hours without amniotic fluid has made it dry and wrinkled, like an old man's. My finger strokes the miniature nose, smaller than my nail, a rounded bump decorated with two nostrils, and then moves to the mouth, the lips moving gently as I touch them; they are moist and soft, with a purple undertone. Though I am afraid to move, I draw him closer to me and kiss his forehead, his little nose, his sweet cheek, his curved lips.

Voices travel from the corridor, there are quick steps, and

then unclear cries. There is something secluded about this room, as if it were some remote annex. In spite of the noise, only my son and I are here, embracing, my tears dropping on his warm cheek. I admire his hands, like doll's hands created by a skilful artist. Every detail is perfect: the joints, the fingers, the nails. The small foot stretches as I touch it, apparently tickling is unpleasant, his face twitches, but then immediately relaxes.

I dare to sit straight on the couch, holding him in my arms, I can't turn my gaze away from him, I watch him breathing, his chest moving lightly. I tighten the blanket, straighten the small hat, my finger touches one eyebrow, then the other, and then—

The eyelids flicker, the eyelashes are so thin that the slightest disturbance in the air moves them, his eyes slowly open and he looks at me, examining me with a pure, bewildered stare. Enchanted, I look at the blue eyes, my heart pounding and my hands slightly shaking, yet I sit still. Overwhelming joy nearly spoils the moment, it almost makes me prefer a strong embrace to silence. So we look into each other's eyes, wonder and amazement interlace with motherly love, light blue eyes, wide open, facing big brown eyes, full of tears, and suddenly, I don't know why, I find myself saying, "Tomer, mummy loves you." As I bend forward to kiss him I see his eyes are closed again, yet contentment is spreading on his small face.

*

I'm glad I got some fresh air. In spite of the buzz from the street, people hastily walking by me (an ambulance siren startling passers-by), walking out of the hospital always brings some relief. I have left the world of the sick and crippled, and emerged onto a noisy street, full of healthy people with busy daily routines. The sun is shining, the sky is cloudless, the light breeze of a spring morning gently sways the treetops.

I sat in a coffee shop right outside the hospital. Two women were sitting next to me, immersed in a conversation about a certain doctor, expressing doubts about whether his medical knowledge could be trusted. On the other side of me an elderly couple were grumbling about an inappropriate medical treatment. Strangely, these conversations brought me some relief. When I left Daphne I felt as though the cries of the labour were still surrounding me, though she had already been resting in another room, waiting for the nurse to bring the baby. In the coffee shop the screams began to fade, blending in with mundane conversations on medical treatment. I sat comfortably, ordered some cake, a cup of coffee, a cold drink, and began to read a newspaper that had been left on one of the tables. I skimmed through the headlines and the political commentary, but as I got to the sport section I began reading a piece about Barcelona and their chances in the Champions League, and when I was done I realized that I had been sitting there for almost an hour.

A sort of inner dispute made me waver about whether I should return to Daphne or stay there for a while. I ordered another cup of coffee, drank it slowly, then paid and began to walk back. On the way I stopped next to a newsstand browsing, and only after a couple of minutes kept walking, and as I entered the hospital I thought I might rest for another couple of minutes in the waiting room. Fear that remnants of the delivery haven't vanished completely kept me from returning to Daphne's room: a pain I had never seen before, screams that cannot be silenced, a body shivering involuntarily. I couldn't return to the room.

I closed my eyes, my head leaning against the wall, wondering what had happened here. How did the birth of a first-born son turn into such a terrifying memory?

For a moment I felt I was the one who was ejected into the world: I am expected to simply become a father, to hold the baby naturally, care for him, support Daphne and look after her. No one is asking me if I am tired, if I would like to have some food, perhaps rest on the sofa. No one is suggesting that I sleep for a couple of hours. All I hear are demanding voices, asking that I cooperate, encourage, strengthen, watch. All I want is to cover my head with a blanket and fall asleep.

Daphne must be waiting for me. I got up, stretched, and began walking towards her room. A male nurse is pushing an old woman in a wheelchair, a group of doctors rush to the lift, a young boy holding his mother's hand is crying, the corridors were covered with colourful landscape paintings. I advanced slowly, planning what I would say, how I would adopt a gentle tone, perhaps even humorous, anything that would make the vestiges of the delivery disappear and drive the desperation out of her eyes. I approached the room, the door was slightly open, perhaps someone had walked in and left it open. I tread carefully, push the door, and then—

Daphne was sitting on the couch, holding the baby in her arms. As I walked in she turned her gaze at me, her eyes were bright, full of light and bliss. There was a hint of a smile on her lips, and in spite of profound exhaustion there was something smooth and radiant about the fair skin, surrounded by long red hair. She caressed the infant cautiously, straightening the bizarre cap on his head, and he slept on her bosom, moving his lips, slightly stretching his tiny hand, as though he was trying to touch an enveloping that is no longer there.

"Tomer, his name is Tomer," she said softly. "I know we haven't decided yet, but I found myself calling him by this name, I don't know why. And now it can't be changed."

She fondled his cheek tenderly, kissed his forehead. A mother and her newborn son, her face was full of innocence and grace, for a moment I thought she was glowing, a beam of light was filling the room and encircling me as well. Carefully I took Tomer into my arms, anxious not to drop him, embraced him and kissed the warm, velvety cheek.

Five Days after the Delivery

Seen from the balcony on the twelfth floor, the buildings of Tel Aviv resemble small toy blocks that were not stacked properly: the lines are not straight, the spaces are not equal, the colours are not uniform or harmonious. The sea is on the other side, and at this late evening hour it puts on its most beautiful gown, light grey but not quite silver, refined and spiritual, airy and soft. Soon the sky will darken and the sea will adopt a bluish-grey colour, slightly metallic, majestic and sombre, which later will transform into eerie, enigmatic black.

Guy remained at our apartment. I left. I am staying with my mother for a couple of days, until I find a new place. I asked Guy to pack my things and send them here. I find everything sickening. I am constantly nauseous. I loathe the balcony, the smell of the sea, the food sent from restaurants, the expensive linens covering my bed. I want to go away, but I don't know where. Maybe I'll go to Europe. A week or two in London, that would comfort me. The music on the radio is dull, the newspaper is disturbing. Yesterday I decided to visit a friend in Haifa. I drove all the way, but when I got there I decided to return to Tel Aviv.

I am standing in the bathroom, facing the mirror, and I

pull up my shirt. Two scratches cross my chest: one has dried blood, the other is thin and pink, stretching from my left breast to the upper abdomen. I inspect each one from side to side, and then I pull down my shirt and wash my face again and again. The face reflected in the mirror looks strange: small eyes, with apparent despair, a mixture of hatred and composure, round face, slightly childish, but the corner of the mouth betrays a certain spasm, a twitch typical of old people, like a distorted smile.

That damn baby, the small creature that everyone is gazing at with such amazement, as if he were the first child ever to come into this world. The ridiculous excitement created by the delivery. The silly smiles and the ludicrous voices they use as they look at him, making faces as if this was the way to show affection. The giggling, the comments about the new parents. I find it all disgusting. Soon I will go to sleep. Another couple of glasses of wine and everything will blur and vanish.

And Guy's urging that we go see the baby together, like a child who believes that if he only tries hard enough everything will work. But it has all been laid out, clear and simple, I don't want children and he doesn't want to give up on becoming a father. Why drag me to the hospital, make me look at the baby, smiling until my face hurts? I have no part in this celebration. I find it alien and unwelcome, everyone invites me to this gathering but I see through the invitation which it is intended to shake an inner conviction, to convince me of what they see as the only truth. Here, I will pour myself another glass of wine.

But he insisted. "Come with me to the hospital to see the baby, I feel uncomfortable going by myself." As if this was a reason we should go together. I should have said no. And his wanting to have sex before we go, preposterous! The way he walked into the bathroom while I took a shower, pretending to be driven by a burning desire, though it was clearly all planned in advance. A charade, annoying but also a bit funny, first I let him pull me onto the bed and stroke me diligently. I saw a green branch through the window, tweeting birds clinging to it, moving their heads from side to side with sudden, quick movements. I then realized that the curtain, made of gossamer fabric that I brought from Italy, was slightly torn. But he insisted, until I ran out of patience. I pushed him back and got on top of the tanned muscular body, ignoring his surprised, anxious gaze, which then became blank and distant, withdrawing into himself in pleasure.

Daphne and Amir's parents were all smiling and excited, when I saw them I wanted to turn back, run to the exit and escape. My presence there with the family was so embarrassing and pointless. And Daphne's mother, looking at me and winking at Guy, said sarcastically that "life is not full until one has children, every woman wants children, it's natural," haughty and vain, examining us. But I could have taken it all, the insults, the eyes following me closely, searching for a hint of envy or tears. I could even take Daphne's mother asking me with feigned kindness if I would like to hold him, as though she was holding a seductive candy and she allows me to taste it. I could have ignored it all, pretended that I somehow found myself in the wrong place, with unfitting company. But Guy approached me and stood behind me. I could feel his eyes following me. He lightly touched my arm, a gentle tap, almost imperceptible, hinting at the new-born's grace and the promise of happiness he carries, as if I have never seen a baby before. *Here, see how cute he is, making his parents so happy.*

I stopped myself from turning around and hitting him. Terrible rage overpowered me, tears filled my eyes, the insult, the rejection, the contempt, I couldn't stand there anymore. In an instant I turned around and ran away, sobbing out loud, ignoring voices calling me. People in the corridor looked at me as I ran not knowing where, until I found the toilet.

The woman in the mirror is so distorted. I can't look at her, I find her repulsive. Small empty eyes, holes in her face, thin tightened lips, an ugly shapeless body, neither girl nor woman, neither thin nor heavy, she has a young boy's face. She is impaired: she will never have children. It's better this way, she hates children. There is something faulty in her, a malfunction that can't be fixed, what others find attractive she finds disgusting. Where others are hungry, she is cold; where others yearn, she fixes her clothing. I will scratch her, maybe pain will awaken a hidden feeling, perhaps this will make the damn motherly instinct emerge. Here, she is bleeding and the blood stains her shirt, small dark spots gradually spreading, like buttons, creating a pattern on the fabric. Pain is so pleasant.

Daddy left us, he lives in the sky now. It is not your fault. Daddy will never come back. But who will take care of us now? What will we do if we need anything? *Don't worry, we will take care of ourselves, everything will be okay.* But what happens if we fail? What will we do? *We will be fine, don't worry, we have money and we will manage. I will take care of you.* But what happens if you're sick and need help? Who will take care of me then? *You know what, let's take care of each other, I will help you and you will help me.*

Another glass of wine, why not? The phone keeps ringing, Guy is calling time and again, he wants to know how I am. I sit on the porch and stare at the sea and wonder when the sun will finally disappear and its light vanish, and the only thing that will be seen is white foam of waves upon a vibrant, animated black sea.

*

Strange to wake up like this, without feeling Abigail breathing next to me. The pillow is smooth, the bed sheet is straight, there are no empty glasses of wine on the bedside table; out of habit I turn around, surprised not to find the dishevelled hair, almost fully covered with a blanket. Even at this early morning hour, it is still dark outside and only night birds' cries are heard, it seems like a strange wind is blowing through the place. I look around as if I found myself in a hotel, wondering why the room is decorated in such a homey manner. A blossoming jasmine, the smell of spring that creeps in is so oppressive; I wish it were raining hard now, and a wind would sway the tree tops so they would sigh heavily.

I lock the door and put the key in my shorts' pocket. When I go out to the street two cats in heat stand facing each other, their calling sounds like weeping; even though I pass right next to them, they remain motionless and do not flee. My feet hurt, my knees are stiff, the thigh muscles are strained, but in a minute they will relax, and the different organs will begin to move in coordination. I run down the street, turn left, and after a couple of minutes I reach the seaside. Early morning rays begin to illuminate the sky but the sea is still dark, and a warm wind blows on the beach. I turn north, feet pounding, one after the other: my breathing rhythm is not quite steady yet, Abigail must still be sleeping, the soft eyebrows, thin eyelashes decorate the small closed eyes, and the hair, which during the day is styled in a modern short cut, is now rumpled—a naughty wild girl!

My feet adjust to an inner pace, matching my fast breathing, carrying my body easily; the pleasure of speed always intoxicating, but I keep feeling the key in my pocket moving from side to side, as if it were very heavy. The apartment that suddenly looks strange, the daily routine that has gone awry, the anticipated phone call from Abigail, it is all so gloomy, so oppressive. I think the only possible cure is jogging. Maybe I will keep running even further than Tel Baruch beach. It's hard to take Abigail's pain. It is the lack of tears, the restrained sadness blended with self-hatred, which is so hard to bear. She acts as if she always knew this would happen. Strange, when we met it was difficult to guess that such desperation lingered underneath the bold feminine appearance. The designer clothes—always walking rapidly on high-heels!—and the childlike smile spreading on a mouth covered with bold red lipstick, it all seemed charming yet balanced, revealing a refined hedonistic spirit, one that leaves no room for such sadness.

Light begins to emerge, low waves approach the shore and recede, a pleasant breeze replaces the warm air. Stride after stride, breath after breath, sweat dripping down my back, the key swinging in my pocket. I run on the wooden deck of the old port and advance northward. Her mother, a strange woman, I find it surprising she doesn't protest her decision not to have children. In spite of her kindness, the way she welcomes every guest warmly, there is something reserved about her. Ridiculously sticking to a certain routine, the appointment with the hairdresser on Thursday, meeting two friends at the local coffee shop every morning, the preparations before the cleaning lady comes, I have never known her break it, not even when I invited her, just like that, spontaneously, for breakfast with Abigail and me. She is a smart and gifted woman, living a comfortable life, nothing more. Maybe if her husband hadn't left her so much of a fortune a hidden vitality would have surfaced, but her prosperous life made her adopt a kind of constant complacency. Who knows, perhaps she suffers from not working more than meets the eye, maybe she secretly regrets the turbulences she never had, the efforts she never made; maybe it isn't family she lacks, but achievements.

The small rise at the very end of Tel Baruch beach is always exhausting, a low dune I wouldn't have felt if I were walking, but now it breaks the rhythm of my breath—here, another couple of steps, I turn around and begin to run back. The sun is shining, the sea is calm, bright and soft, azure distances moving in the morning breeze.

When Amir asked me why we broke up I said I want children and Abigail doesn't. But I found this simple and reasonable answer so annoying. I kept explaining and elaborating and Amir kept saying, "Yes, of course, I understand," nodding in agreement. Her career, growing up without a father, her mother who always felt out of place, the money that made life comfortable but not productive, more and more explanations, fully compatible with each other yet somehow irrelevant, ignoring the main thing, concealing an obscure feeling that I am missing something, a deprivation I don't fully understand. After all, before Daphne got pregnant the idea of becoming a father was completely abstract, a theoretical possibility without any concrete details. Years ago, the night Abigail told me she didn't want to have children, I was staring at the ceiling, tired and absent minded, and I fell asleep after a minute or two.

"I don't understand why I am so frustrated," I told Amir, who simply said, "I think it's very clear why."

I pass the old port just coming back to life at this early morning hour and keep going southwards. The coastline curves and then straightens again, I am close to the end of my run. The anger within me resurfaces, after almost an hour of running the emptiness is still there, not only did it not dissipate but it grew more tangible. The comforting power of jogging fell short this time; I was expecting the relief at the end of the run but found nothing but exhaustion, a deepening despair, accentuated by the physical effort.

Suddenly out of anger an idea pops up: I will run as fast as I can until the place I stop, push myself to the very end, pretend that I am taking part in a race and I am about to win. If I can get in front of my competitor—I will break a record. Last sprint, and I'll be the winner. In spite of my aching leg muscles and the heavy panting I speed up as if I had just begun running. I am surprised how fast I can run; it is invigorating, removing the emptiness, replacing it with a strange exaltation. Others observe me amazed, for people rarely speed like that on the beach. I pass one man, a woman, there are just a couple of metres left, and suddenly, in this fast motion, I understand, truly understand, what it is that I am denied: Abigail won't let me be unlike my father. There is nothing I want more than to be a different husband, a different father, to separate myself from him, to be a person of an altogether different nature. But Abigail is stopping me, forcing a distance between us. Saying she doesn't want children makes me a temporary partner, even if she won't admit it. This is what my father was: a temporary partner. A companion for an adventure, good time, sex; a person no one expects to find after an hour, a day, a year. And if he did show up, everybody knew he is about to disappear soon, or would find another companion. I am out of breath. I must stop.

When I get home I'll call Amir. I wonder what he will think about it? I remove my socks quickly, toss my shoes on the sand, and unlike my usual self I dash into the water, skipping over small waves in shallow water and swim deeper into the sea.

Tenth Month

"Daphne, why aren't you sleeping?"

"I want to make sure Tomer is okay."

"He's sound asleep. Everything is fine. You should get some rest, you're so tired."

"Is he breathing? Are you sure he is breathing? I don't see his chest moving."

"He's sleeping soundly, that's all."

"I'm not sure. Yes, everything is fine. For a moment..."

"I find myself doing the same thing several times a day."

"Yes, me too."

"Don't you want to go to sleep? If he wakes I will give him a bottle. There is some advantage in not breastfeeding."

"Stop it, I told you I can't breastfeed. I accept the fact that it is good for Tomer's health, but I simply can't."

"You know, I don't really care, I mean I'm sure he will turn out to be a healthy boy—but I simply can't understand it. Did you find it disgusting?"

"Not at all!"

"Was it painful?"

"Painful? Not exactly. Not in a physical way."

"I don't understand."

"It is hard to explain it. It was as if he were sucking me from myself. I find it strange that breastfeeding is a symbol of prosperity, of growth. I felt this elixir was taken from me. Every small suck left me emptier. I felt life was drained from me."

"Strange. I know it is healthier for the baby to be breastfed, but I guess the main thing is that he will be a source of joy, not suffering."

"I can't do it. Maybe other women feel differently, for me it was torture."

"I'm sure he will develop well with formula milk. He is so cute, isn't he?"

"Adorable."

"Looking around curiously."

"Wonderful."

"And such an intelligent look."

"Looking at the world with amazement."

"He is pretty tall for his age."

"And so handsome."

"Guy says he looks like you. Strange, since he and Abigail broke up he shrinks away from Tomer. It seemed like the birth sparked something in him, he even dared hold him in his arms. Now he smiles at him distantly and keeps away. I wonder why."

"I'm sorry they broke up. I really liked Abigail. I don't understand why she didn't want to have children. Ever since Tomer was born I'm eager to have more children."

"Maybe it's not right for everyone. Guy never thought of having children, and he wasn't looking for a partner to be a mother. Your pregnancy sparked something. You know, his father was never at home, even when his parents were married. Guy hates him, though they often meet. I always wondered if he would eventually live like him, in spite of his utter repugnance for whatever his father does. A couple of weeks ago he phoned me early in the morning, after jogging, and told me that he had finally figured out why he was angry at Abigail: she was stopping him from being different from his father. Her decision not to be a mother makes him a temporary partner, not a life-long one."

"Why does he dislike his father so much?"

"His dad always cheated on his mother and didn't even bother to hide it. After the divorce he dated numerous women. Guy once told me that they arranged to meet at a coffee shop, and as he got there he saw his father sitting there fondling a young woman. He simply turned around and walked away, and hasn't spoken to him in nearly a year."

"Why did his father cheat on his mother like that?"

"Why do people cheat on their partners?! I don't know. I always thought it contains a seed of hatred."

"Hatred? For whom? For their partner?"

"Their partner, themselves, maybe their whole lives, I don't know. People pick one way to live and then wish they'd chosen another. They commit to the woman they love and then dislike her because she stops them being with anyone else. So maybe cheating is about finding if it is possible to change some choices. Not that we want to change them; we simply want to know it's possible."

"Maybe it's simply falling for someone?"

"Obviously, but it's not just about that. It's a taste of the life you will never have: a romance with a woman you won't live with, a body you won't see age, family and friends you won't meet. The enchantment is the risk; not the risk of getting caught, but that the person you are cheating with would turn out to be better than your partner. And this ongoing comparison—Daphne, are you crying? I can't see in the dark, are you crying?"

"No, only a couple of tears. It happens quite often lately."

"Daph, you know I am not talking about myself, don't you? Come here, let me hug you. I was only imagining how it must feel. You know how happy I am with us and Tomer, don't you?"

"I'm just a bit moody lately."

"I know. Maybe we should consult the doctor? Perhaps it's postpartum depression."

"Maybe. I don't know what that really means."

"A physical consequence of giving birth, an imbalance that produces depression. I read about it."

"Imbalance? Between what? I think it is all the result of pain."

"The result of pain?"

"Yes. Never have I experienced such torment. You know, all my life I have been afraid of the pain of giving birth. This fear, a vague, fundamental anxiety, has always been there, without needing any special attention. A sort of understanding that something I want dearly will necessarily involve terrible agony. And this comprehension mars even the happiest expectations of the future."

"Were you always nervous about giving birth?"

"Yes. And from the moment I knew I was pregnant the fear became real, fully tangible, a petrifying feeling that leaves no room for other emotions."

"Well, I am glad the labour is over. Now is the time for happiness."

"Ah, well, this is what I didn't understand: the fear of the birth is one side of the coin; the other side is the actual experience of pain."

"I don't understand."

"I discovered that the torment generated a new, unfamiliar

fragility. Every contraction tearing my body created a new kind of meekness, every exploding vein produced self-doubt—I found that pain truly makes you see yourself, demonstrating your frailty, leaving you feeble, distrusting yourself. The night after the delivery, when the suffering was fresh and the wound still bleeding, I cried in bed, overwhelmed by my physical weakness, my failure to hold back, the marks torture left even when pain itself had subsided, and for the first time in my life I saw myself in all my weakness. I always thought I was an optimistic person, willing to make any effort to overcome obstacles. But after the birth I realized pain could break me down in an instant: one contraction, the body is torn, and all that is left are cries of pain and nothing else. Postpartum depression? No, a different person after giving birth."

"Strange, I never thought about it but that's true."

"Do you know what my mother, my sister, the nurses told me? 'You will soon forget it all.'"

"They're right, aren't they?"

"No, absolutely not. I mean, the memory of pain fades, but not its effect."

"I never could have believed pain has such consequences."

"You know I love Tomer dearly and I'm thrilled that I have a child. But I find this disregard for the suffering of labor infuriating."

"It seems to me it's better to try and forget it all. Anyway it can't be changed."

"I think it's the other way around: the suffering must be respected."

"Respect suffering? Is it good to be in pain?"

"Of course not. I would rather not feel the childbirth at all. But if it involves such torture, it should be acknowledged and appreciated. Simply ignoring it is insulting. It became part of me."

"Daphne, you know what happened to my mother when I was born…"

"Yes."

"I was always angry with her."

"I know."

"It may be that I didn't really understand. Perhaps I'll ask her what exactly happened then. Hey, Tomer is waking up. Come Daphne, look how sweet he is, moving his lips like that."

Twelfth Month

How is it possible to ask such a question? How? Some questions should never be posed to others. They are meant only for yourself, and only you can find a meaningful answer. And if you wish to consult others, even those closest to you – even your own mother – the question would become tasteless and vulgar, creating anger and... distance.

Well, it all began one afternoon with an artless, pleasant conversation when Amir brought Tomer over for a couple of hours so Daphne could get some rest. Since Tomer was sleeping we sat comfortably in the living room, speaking in low voices, careful not to wake him. Warm afternoon breezes filled the room, the trees cast soft shadows on the house, toning down the orange light of an early summer sun. I relaxed in the old leather armchair, leaning my head back, placing my legs on the small footstool with a padded top; Amir took off his sandals and stretched out on the brown sofa.

I feel much better since the birth of my first grandson... an old scab is now peeling away, revealing fresh pinkish skin. Though when Amir called to say they were on their way to the hospital, an evil spirit took hold of me. First I dropped the phone. Then I accidentally knocked over the beautiful vase from the Armenian pottery shop in the Old City of Jerusalem, and it shattered on the floor with an explosive crash. Aaron quickly picked up the pieces, saying "never mind, we'll go there again and get a new one," tossing the decorated pieces into the bin. Finally I hurried to go out, muttering something about some shopping that needed to be done, almost tripping down the stairs. First I went towards the greengrocers. On the way I changed my mind and decided to go to the supermarket. As I got there I realized there was no point anyway, I wouldn't be cooking now. I went up and down the street, feeling my heart beat, and pacing in confusion, an agitation that wasn't directed at anything but that spins around and can't find any rest. Finally I found myself once again at the synagogue...

This time I went directly to the women's section and sat in the front row. The cantor's voice filled the place, and a couple of elderly women were praying silently, looking down at the *Siddur*, turning the pages. Someone offered me a prayer book, but I held up my palm in rejection. I wasn't interested in those ancient verses praising God, begging for salvation or counting on his promises. I was looking for the limited spirit of the synagogue, an acknowledgment of life's turmoil without assuming or pretending it was unexpected.

I sat there for two hours, my eyes closed as I listened to the prayers, feeling from afar how the birth of my grandson was taking place, independent of me. Finally I got up and went home. A couple of minutes after I got there Amir called to tell us a beautiful healthy grandson was born.

But since Tomer's birth an old pain is fading, and a blessed happiness takes its place. Every time I hold him another tiny piece of oppressive memory is washed away, replaced by a small portion of the present. I feed him, change his nappy, put him to bed: the blue eyes, the small nose, the protruding lips, a chubby hand stretching up every time he eats, his first smile... which spread on his face as he was looking at me of all people! They all obscure the past to the point that it seems as though it must soon disappear...

As Amir and I relaxed in the living room that late afternoon, Tomer sleeping in the small crib next to us, one would have thought that the old memories could be spread out without creating too much unhappiness.

Amir told me how his boss, Mr. Schuster, had appeared unexpectedly in his office. Dressed in his usual shabby suit, he shook Amir's hand and saying, "Mazel tov, I'm glad to hear you have a boy", patted him on his back and disappeared before Amir could answer. "He probably came just to check if I was working", Amir grinned, adding that everyone knows Mr. Schuster ensures that no one leaves early. He then told me that Daphne went to visit the welfare office with Tomer, and all the social workers, including the older ones, circled around him and smiled as if they have never seen a baby before. She's hesitating about whether she should return to work or extend her maternity leave. Although he was talking casually a hint of embarrassment came into his eyes and he said, nonchalantly, that Daphne thinks that the pain of childbirth has far-reaching consequences that are not fully acknowledged. She believes, so he said, that they are the source of what is called "postpartum depression," and in general she feels that she is a different person since the birth.

Silence spread through the room. Amir was holding a soft toy, turning it from side to side, looking at it without daring to so much as glance at me. I closed my eyes, wondering why he mentioned Daphne's words... His tone was not angry, but who knows, maybe it concealed an accusation. I hesitated whether I should answer, but the silence in the room clearly indicated that he had no interest in any small talk. So I began by saying that I certainly agree with Daphne, and waited for his response. As I saw him now turn from the toy to me, waiting, I said that my labour with him was very unusual even in those days, and it certainly wouldn't have taken place today. But in a way it wasn't entirely different from most deliveries, only more extreme. The unbearable pain that lasted for hours made the emotional response more acute. But still, I agree with Daphne, the suffering of childbirth makes a woman a different person, even if after a couple of weeks it all seems to have been forgotten. "In fact," I said, "I don't think this feeling is limited to childbirth. I've heard that people who undergo substantial physical pain report a mental change. But for some reason, when it comes to delivery, everyone, including women, say it is 'forgotten,' 'buried,' 'erased.'"

Amir was sitting upright on the sofa. His posture was tense and stiff. He stared at me, eyebrows furrowed, mouth clenched, biting his lower lip as he does when he's trying to solve a problem. Weighing every word, listening to the unspoken ones, I felt he could even hear my shortening breath. As I fell silent he said: "Frankly, it makes sense, but I really can't understand how pain can change a person to the point that she can't perform as a parent."

A little rustle was coming from the crib. We both looked at it: perhaps Tomer had woken up. No, he was only moving in his sleep.

I wanted to answer but I didn't know what to say. I wished to explain, justify, ease his distress, but an unfamiliar anger began to bubble, a new resentment was revealed, exposed after Tomer's birth. Maybe instead of asking me time and again how the delivery ruined my maternal functioning he could say he was sorry for my anguish, express some sympathy for my pain. A father himself, he has seen how difficult a normal, healthy birth is. One would have expected some compassion, some appreciation for the torment of bringing a child into this world, especially with a very difficult labour. I have had enough of this self-justification... I didn't choose to have such a difficult delivery, and what followed it was beyond my control. When the doctor at the psychiatric ward asked me why I thought the labour had affected me in such a way, I replied that I didn't know, perhaps the labour blurred the fact that I was an adult and made me a child again – she is in pain and no one is helping her, she begs for relief and no one is listening...

"Well, Amir, now that you are a father, isn't it about time that you look at what you call 'the trauma of my birth' in a more mature manner? Even if it shaped your first years, still it can't be the cause for everything. A man has to take some responsibility for his life, don't you think?"

A glimmer of anger filters into his gaze, an age old exasperation twitches on Amir's face, which betrays unfamiliar exhaustion in this late afternoon light.

"We have often discussed this. Clearly a child would be affected if the mother is unable to embrace him. I don't blame you, I see where it is coming from, but I still find it strange that it had such a profound effect."

I found his response infuriating. I have never felt this way. I always try to explain how in spite of the fact that I returned home when he was a couple of months old, I loved him with all my heart from the very first moment. I elaborated how Aaron's devotion compensated for my absence. But now I was annoyed. His wife had explained how hard a normal birth is, even without any complications, yet he keeps blaming me.

"I know you think my difficulties created your emotional problems, but isn't it a way of not taking responsibility for your life? Perhaps it is a way of justifying some unfortunate choices?"

"What choices?"

"I don't know."

"Marrying Daphne?"

"God, no! I love her with all my heart."

"Me too. Still, I cheat on her."

"What?"

"Yes. A sort of mental distortion, I have no other explanation. A desire to destroy a relationship of deep love."

"Cheating on her? I don't believe you. With who?"

"What does it matter? Someone. I know her from college. I was unfaithful when she was pregnant, and I still am. What do you think? Don't you think it is a bit crazy?"

"Amir, are you telling me the truth? Do you really cheat on Daphne?"

"Yes."

"Why? I simply can't understand it. She is a wonderful young woman."

"Yes. I love her very much. But still, the pregnancy created a need to stand apart, to behave as if it had nothing to do with me. I don't know if I was afraid that the delivery would go wrong, or certain that it would be fine, and life would take an irreversible turn. And also, I thought Daphne wasn't happy at all with being pregnant. Maybe I was angry, I wanted to get back at her."

"For God's sake, Amir, I simply can't believe it. How did this happen to you?"

"It's terrible. I know. I want to ask Daphne for

forgiveness. What do you say, should I tell her?"

"Are you asking me if you should tell her?"

"Yes."

"You want me to decide if you should confess to your wife that you cheated on her while she was pregnant?"

"Yes."

"What kind of question is it? You are the only one who can decide what to do."

"Why? I am asking for your help."

"I am sorry, Amiri. It is your decision. You are on your own here, and no one can help you, not even those closest to you. Why have you done this? May God forgive me if I am to blame for this... Honestly, I couldn't have done anything differently after your birth. Maybe if I were a stronger person everything would have been different. But I collapsed; not in body but in soul."

*

Shame, it's such a shame that Amir is pouring poisonous drops into our happiness, depriving Rebecca of the joy she so truly deserves. Anyway, he will do whatever he wants, regardless of her advice. But time and again he tries to make her apologize, to confess. It makes me so sad. I thought that when he would become a father this miserable need to justify his bitterness, his sense of deprivation, would finally disappear. But he keeps pressing her, trying to extract something that would defend his character, prove that it is not his fault that he is so often driven by envy.

Since Tomer was born a new spirit prevails here. Now that Rebecca has become a grandmother she quietly hums tunes as she washes the dishes, fills the fridge with delicacies she never bought before, buys flowers every Friday. It seems like a tight knot has suddenly unravelled. No longer is she infuriated by noise coming from the first floor, no longer does she grumble about high prices. Mellow songs are coming from the radio, a bright tablecloth with a cheerful design is spread across the kitchen table, and the small window at the far end of the living room, which was always covered with dark blinds, is open now, letting new, unfamiliar light into the room.

Even the weekly meeting with her friends has almost become a nuisance. For years they met in a coffee shop in the centre of Tel Aviv, four women who have known each other for a long time. Their conversation, so Rebecca has told me, develops in two possible channels: talk about their children and grandchildren, each one sharing the joys and troubles of the others; or they grumble together about bad service, a disappointing doctor, overpriced products. If a complaint is direct and explicit, they all join the general discontent; but if it is only implicit and indirect, one friend might add that maybe it could be seen in a different light, perhaps it is not rudeness or bad intentions but only a misunderstanding. The young waitress serves them faithfully, confident that she will be rewarded.

But since the delivery Rebecca isn't eager to meet with them. At first she avoided the meeting, saying she must help Daphne and Amir. Then she was late, apologizing and saying she had to buy baby products. Later, as they met in the coffee shop, she began to dress differently. Though in spite of her age she has kept her girlish figure, her appearance used to be— well, severe, almost lacking any adornment. Clothes made of dark fabric—at most she would add a scarf. But lately she draws out of the wardrobe dresses I never knew she had: tight, bright, emphasizing her narrow waistline. When she stood at the door on her way to meet "the girls," her hair swept aside in an unusual manner and her lips covered with red lipstick, I smiled at her and said: "Maybe you would rather stay here with me?"

Before my retirement from the bank I had an interesting conversation with the branch manager, a tall, bold man, with heavy glasses, always troubled by the next inspection. A couple of weeks after his first grandchild had been born he invited the senior clerks to his office for a toast. "So, what is it like to be a grandfather?" I asked him. He took off his glasses, wiped the sweat off his forehead with a handkerchief, and said, "You won't believe it, it's like travelling back in time. I don't understand why people feel old when they become grandparents. I think it is the other way around. Creating a new generation produces vigour and renewed happiness, a sort of support to one's ability to procreate."

I looked at him, wondering if the rumours of his two mistresses were true. He always seemed so troubled by managing the branch, I found his referring to his virility bizarre.

But since Tomer was born I realize there was some truth in his words. Already after the birth, full of excitement, Rebecca and I held hands for a long time. She normally sleeps in the bedroom, I fall asleep in what used to be Amir's room. But then, elated and exhausted, we went together to the bedroom and fell asleep in each other's arms. Well, we now sleep together again. After the initial excitement of the delivery subsided, a new passion emerged. Not restored youth, but on the contrary, a revived old age. A new encounter with our ageing bodies.

At first I was anxious, worried that the signs of age would be unattractive. But surprisingly I found they generated empathy. Sagging skin, wrinkles, creases time had created, I began to see them as manifestations of our life together. And so my own imperfections became bearable, even natural. Pure happiness filled me when I found a beauty spot at the base of her left breast—I had almost forgotten it was there. Two elderly people who have managed to complete a life cycle, to bring into this world not only a son but also a grandson, are now getting reacquainted with their bodies with acceptance and a touch of joy, old age with some gratification. Oh, it is strange and lovely.

But now that I overheard Rebecca and Amir I was anxious again. I feared that the new ease, miraculously created at the age of almost seventy, would disappear, and might be replaced again by sadness disguised as hectic housework, grumbling about inefficiencies, or excessive concern about money. I entered the room only when Amir was standing at the door, carrying Tomer in a car seat. I said my farewells and kissed Tomer, who closed his eyes as my face approached him, and opened them only when he was sure I had stepped back. As the door closed I turned anxiously to Rebecca, wondering if she would lower her gaze again and mumble that she couldn't have done anything differently. But to my utter surprise she looked at me with those almond eyes that haven't lost their brightness over the years, smiled and said: "He is simply adorable, don't you think? Did you see how he smiled at me? Every time he sees me his smiles. What an angel!" I sighed with relief, lightly caressing her arm, admitting that I had overheard their conversation.

"I am sorry both for him and for her. It is such a shame that he ruins his life like that. But it is about time he overcame this immature brooding. Even if I am to blame for his faults, he is now a father, a married man, a successful accountant, why does he insist on clinging to what he thinks justifies whatever he does? But there is no such thing as pardon in advance for whatever you do. You know it hurts me, but it's better that this illusion should end, that he understands that pretending he has an emotional justification is not only lacking but mainly limiting. Wouldn't it be better to simply admit he failed to conquer his desires? To resist temptation?"

"Yes, I think it is much better. But people of his generation almost never admit it. I think Daphne would have used simpler, more direct words."

Fourteenth Month

I find it peculiar that moments of utter happiness always contain the seeds of hidden anxiety. It is as though bliss contains its very opposite, the way courage has some fear, or curiosity has ignorance. When Tomer sits on the floor facing me, his small legs spread apart and his body swaying slightly from side to side, trying to keep his balance, looking at me and smiling, the happiness that fills me is so complete, yet deep within there is also fear. His huge eyes, that have gradually transformed from blue to brown, are full of laughter, and he keeps burbling *bbbbbbbb*, banging the small soft toy with the tiny bell on the floor, enjoying the little ring, and then throwing it aside and looking at me intently, waiting to see if I will laugh or utter syllables in a reproachful tone.

When I see he is about to fall back I catch him, and he holds his arms up, waiting for me to lift him. I take him in my arms and he hugs me and puts his lips against my cheek, licks it and wets it, a baby's kiss that he knows will produce cries of joy. Cuddling, we walk to the kitchen. I pick up a bottle of milk, and together we sprawl on the sofa in the living room. When he sees the bottle he opens his mouth wide and moves his hands and legs restlessly, eager to seize it. As the nipple reaches his mouth his body relaxes in an instant, and he stares blankly at an invisible spot in the room.

I close my eyes, careful not to fall asleep while he is drinking. Fatigue is the best cure for the last few months' turbulence; tiredness counterbalances exaltation and gloom, joy and desperation; it moderates fierce emotions, directing all excitement onto a narrow, well-defined path, with a predetermined end. It is impossible to be consumed by anger when all you want is to get into bed and fall asleep. And concern about Tomer's development, or the fear of him having an unknown disease, are easily reduced by an incessant need to nap. He wakes up three times a night. I feed him twice, Amir feeds him once. At night Tomer's eyes are wide open as he looks into the darkness with curiosity. When I look at him he smiles, reaching out his hand and touching my face as if he is blind: eyes, nose, mouth. When he is finished with the bottle he takes a pacifier. He then stares at the room like he's never seen it before. After a couple of minutes, the eyelids flutter and thin lashes cover the big eyes. I sit still, careful not to wake him. Only when I see he is fast asleep do I carry him carefully to his bed.

Yesterday I went again to the welfare office. I was hoping to meet with the director, to find out under what conditions I can return to work. Since I have already regained my pre-pregnancy figure, I put on my favourite grey dress, tight yet casual. As I was standing at the door I felt there was something shabby about my appearance. I looked in the mirror, trying to spot the weariness I thought I had seen. All of a sudden I realized I had grown a little old; the freshness of youth, revealed in an obscure way, was gone. The eyes, the neck, the breasts, they all seemed very feminine yet in an unfamiliar way. I decided to wear another necklace and put on burgundy lipstick. But as I looked again in the mirror I realized that they changed nothing, they recovered no youth.

Gal and Rotem greeted me with unrestrained excitement, hugging me and asking after Tomer: *Well, what is he like now? What can he do? Does he say "mummy"? Why didn't you bring him along? Come on, let's see the pictures.* I sat in the corner at my old desk, which was still smooth and dark, nothing on it in spite of no extra space in the room; no doubt they kept it empty, emphasizing that I was missed. Rotem grabbed my cell phone and rummaged through the photos, smiling happily, saying from time to time: "So cute" or "he looks exactly like you." Gal made me a cup of coffee, inquiring about Tomer, about me, when will I return to work? Her obvious kindness almost brought me to tears. Her concern about others, the attention to minor details, the wish to offer the best solution—suddenly I found myself saying: "I don't know what to do, whether I should return to work. I find the idea of leaving Tomer with a stranger rather depressing."

"You must return to work."

"Why?"

"You don't understand the price of staying at home."

"I don't care. I want what is best for Tomer."

"Daphne, I know you feel this way now. But in a year or two everything will be different. Someone will take your position, and it won't be easy to find another job. You simply must return to work."

"I understand what you're saying, but I feel there is something so wrong about a baby this age unable to be with his parents. Not only the mother, but the father as well. But Amir can't miss a minute of work. I think he would be rather happy to take care of Tomer a couple of mornings every week, and work in the afternoons. But it's simply impossible."

"This is also true for you. The welfare office is not open at night!"

"Frankly, it is not a bad idea. I'm sure the 'Aunties' wouldn't like it, but maybe this is the right thing to do. I am sure many parents feel the same, but they have no choice but to find a nanny."

"There is no other choice. This is how it works. You don't want children to go to school in the afternoon, do you?"

"Actually, why not?"

"Listen, Daphne, you may be right. But until a change takes place you need to think of yourself. A person who isn't working is always pushed aside, seen as worthless. It is never spelled out loud, but it is true. When someone will ask you what you do and you will reply 'I'm a mum' or 'I raise my child' you will see people underestimating you."

I was suddenly out of breath. I wasn't sure why. Gal's words were simple and direct, with no pretence. They didn't stem from ideology but from a simple, touching concern for me. Every word she added was oppressive, proving how right she was. For a moment I saw Tomer smiling at me, reaching out his chubby hands, waiting for me to pick him up; but Gal's arguments echoed in the room. She kept explaining how a person's value is almost entirely determined by his or her profession.

When I left the welfare office summer sun showed strong light on the street, full of dust and car fumes. The passers-by, sweating and looking for some shade, walked briskly to escape the heat. The trees had a brownish yellow tone, there were empty beer bottles and old newspapers strewn on street benches, and loud car horns filled the air. The neglect of south Tel Aviv was more apparent under this blazing sun. I walked slowly, thinking about Gal's words, repeating every sentence, both accepting and rejecting them. It is impossible to leave Tomer and impossible to stop working. My gaze lowered, and I strolled blindly along. Suddenly I heard someone calling "Daphne, Daphne."

Green eyes encircled by thick black lashes looked at me with clear joy, straight brown hair fell on the forehead, fair skin—Jonathan was smiling at me. He didn't attempt to conceal his pleasure that we had run into each other. He stood close to me, staring at me, trying to guess my thoughts. A strange stupor took over and immediately faded away. For a moment everyone disappeared, Gal, the welfare office, even Tomer, and I was facing a man who had courted me for years. A thought passes, a successful computer man, talented and imaginative – the years have been good to him. He asked what was I doing in south Tel Aviv, and I replied that I have recently had a baby boy, that I was on maternity leave, that I was not quite sure whether I would return to work. Surprisingly, not only was he not taken aback by me being a mother but he seemed even more enthusiastic, inquiring when exactly was my son born, how old is he now, is he sleeping at night, or rather, do I manage to get some sleep?

He stood next to me and I could smell the scent of his body. A casual, commonplace conversation, but physical attraction gave it a new, somewhat strange twist. Every sentence sounded different, concealing unknown secrets. He was a partner in a successful high-tech company that moved its office to south Tel Aviv. Something about medical robotics. A very interesting topic. He mentioned no wife or children, only hard work. Embarrassment made me toss my hair forward on my chest, and he followed my movements, observing my long hair, almost reaching out and touching it. When he was standing so close to me that I could feel his breath, I recoiled and stepped back, apologized, I needed to go. I left almost without saying goodbye, I walked away briskly, all but running to my car, turning on the engine and beginning to drive. I was so absent minded that I almost hit the car parked next to me. A loud horn was heard as I tried to merge into traffic.

Driving home, I kept thinking about this unexpected meeting. His gaze, following my countenance, the hand that almost touched me, the thin chest hair under the ironed shirt, the modest spirit of a successful man, how had he suddenly shown up in this shabby, heat-stricken street, fresh and smiling? As if an invisible hand had placed him there on purpose to emphasize the sweat and sloppiness of which he has no part. Blue collar workers, exhausted at the end of a workday, a toothless old woman walking slowly while talking to herself, the falafel shop owner whose clothes smell of fried oil, and Jonathan, clean shaven, apparently getting out of a fancy car and into an air-conditioned office. Though he wasn't dressed too elegantly, something about his cleanliness suggested wealth, the comfort of those who do not walk on steamy sidewalks in the summer. And his look of desire, pretending not to examine my body, trying to see through the dress, stirred a forgotten excitement. Unintentionally I recalled last night: Amir treats my body as though it were made of glass, he keeps asking me if he is hurting me, touching me cautiously. Sometimes it seemed he was doing that to fulfil an obligation, re-establishing our being a couple. And so the meekness created by childbirth is expanding, entrenching itself and escalating, creating further self-doubt and sadness.

Jonathan, unlike Amir, is not intimidated by me being a mother. For a moment I thought he would embrace me, kiss me passionately, without needless caution. The intimate tone, the detailed questions about my life, it all seemed so direct and uninhibited.

An unknown caller is calling my cell phone. I answered.

"Daphne, it's me, Jonathan. You see, I managed to find your number. I know you are married, but I really want to meet you. It means a lot to me."

*

I find it disturbing that these moments of self-loathing have become so casual. They used to create tumult, hesitations (door slamming!), even tears. But now they have become mundane; it is normal that a faint but constant nausea is part of my daily routine, and it intensifies before I meet with Sari. When I climb the steps to her flat I want to be punished, I consider what would be a proper punishment, and finally I am angry that no one is punishing me. The injustice makes me grim, and makes Sari laugh to tears.

Her mockery is more explicit and flagrant (she calls me "poodle," asking "how are the wife and baby?"), making my sin more perceptible, unmasking some mysterious and obscure complication in my life. And Daphne's invisible presence has long evaporated. I used to feel she was watching me from a corner, astonished and embarrassed, but now only Sari and I are there, and every meeting becomes more vulgar, humiliating, more full of hatred. I even abhor the sight of her bed, covered with colourful linens, I hate the huge window (that has a rusty hinge), the black and white photo of a modern building: oh, I detest this room.

But there is a strange pleasure in self-hatred, and it makes me return here time and again.

We normally meet at lunchtime. I then rush back to the

office, since I don't want to run into Mr. Schuster on the prowl. A couple of times he saw me walking briskly from the parking lot to the office. He watched me with both distrust and curiosity, clearly he was wondering where I was coming from. Since then his watery eyes follow me more openly and impolitely, he never lowers his gaze when he stares at me. He also throws me additional tasks. Several times he sent for me, asking me to handle files of important clients. Last time, while requesting that I review a certain statement, he added: "This is rather urgent. You may not be able to go out for lunch, as we want this ready on time." I looked at him in surprise, but he, like his usual self, waved his hand, perhaps for goodbye, perhaps suggesting that I should leave. Later that afternoon he walked into my office, inquiring about certain sections of the statement, making sure that I went into every small detail. He then looked at Tomer's photo placed in a silver frame on my desk, turned his watery eyes at me and walked away.

Frankly I prefer to be busy working. Calculating spending and costs, adding numbers, careful not to make mistakes, comparing different articles, delving into small details—it makes thinking about other things almost impossible. When I am tired I look at Tomer's picture: big brown eyes, smart and full of laughter, wearing a blue shirt, gazing at the camera curiously. I touch his pink cheek with my finger. The photo does not convey the sweet smell of his body, the fontanelle that hasn't closed yet, the small fingernails that are so hard to cut since he keeps moving his hands.

Thinking of him makes me smile, but gloom sweeps over me. Maybe if I were spending more time with him all this complication would have ended long ago. If I were taking care of him for several hours every day and not only late in the evening, completely devoted to him, to his laughter and crying, his food and diapers, I wouldn't have had any spare time to explore my defects, my weaknesses. Caring for a baby leaves no room for other things, Daphne keeps saying that. But she is the one who is looking after him, not me. Sometimes it feels as if she lends him to me on evenings and weekends, explaining how to prepare his formula, that the new diapers are more comfortable. If I were the one spending most of the day with him perhaps this void (which Sari fills now) wouldn't have been created, an inner gap that wasn't supposed to open. But it has been created, and I have no idea how else to fill it, how to remove this twisted urge to see myself sinking in repulsive lust.

I realized it was late and decided to call it a day. I arranged the papers in two identical piles, saved the files on the computer, turned off the light and drove home. Traffic was heavy; summer heat slows down the cars even on the wider avenues of Tel Aviv. As I was going up the stairs I could imagine Daphne dressed casually, shorts and a tank top probably, feeding Tomer or perhaps putting him to sleep. I opened the door.

Daphne stood there, all dressed and made up, playing with Tomer and smiling at me. The long hair flowing softly, the elongated figure wrapped in thin fabric.

For a single moment a spark of fire was reflected in the big eyes.

I dropped my briefcase.

I was lost. I was eager to kiss her, but she turned around, bent down, lifted Tomer and carried him as he was banging a toy on her back. As they walked into the nursery room I heard her say: "Guy called. Abigail has won an important international prize for design. Did you know that?"

Sixteenth Month

Autumn. Gone are the summer days, yellow-brown tones, blazing sun, and air saturated with tiny water drops. They are now replaced by a grey transparent light, a cool breeze late in the afternoon and blue-toned clouds emerging from the sea in the evening, assuming dark, alarming shapes. Birds fill the sky on their way to Africa, a flock of feathers flying together to warmer places, spreading their wings and gliding in the air; always some lag behind, exhausted or wounded, those who will not survive the long journey.

My stay in London has done me good. I rented a room on the banks of the Thames, not too elegant but very clean, with a huge window overlooking the water. Every day I sat in a coffee shop right by the riverside. I would stare at the waves, the boats, the tourists coming and going, on the old buildings and St. Paul's Cathedral on the opposite side. The waiters observed me in bewilderment and even inquired several times if I didn't want to tour London. But I surrendered to the soft light, emerging from a gentle sun or filtering through clouds, to the buildings' straight lines perpendicular to the flowing water, to the round dome of St. Paul's above them, and to profound blessed strangeness. Finally there was no need to explain, elaborate, apologize. Clients kept calling me, when would I be back, they are waiting for months with the renovation, but I apologized and referred them to other interior decorators who would be glad to take the job, sorry, I am on an unplanned vacation. Most of them complained, but when I said I am not sure when I'd return asked if there was someone I would recommend. Only one client, a well-known lawyer who had just bought an apartment in a narrow street in the centre of Tel Aviv, kept calling every day, begging me to return and renovate it.

Odd how thoughts travel to unpredicted destinations. I was planning to examine my life, to ponder my decision not to have children, to adopt a serene and disillusioned point of view, without agitation or hesitation. But my thoughts turned to all the houses I had redecorated. One after the other they flashed before my eyes: the materials, the perception of space, lighting, corners, kitchens, I couldn't stop. I started examining the file of each apartment, delving into every detail as if I had been given an opportunity to correct a hidden error which I needed to discover. Beautiful places no doubt, tastefully designed, open spaces and cosy corners, everyone says my work demonstrates perfect harmony. But I kept looking at the photos, re-evaluating every choice, searching for the hidden flaw, which since I came to London I was certain truly exists. Bright walls integrate perfectly with straight-lined furniture, comfortable inviting modern kitchens, quiet bedrooms, almost without embellishment—where did I go wrong? What should have been different?

I was sitting in the coffee shop by the river, deep in thought, as the waitress brought a cup of coffee. An older woman, very friendly, she always chatted with the customers. As she saw me turning off the computer and looking at the view she said: "You know, dear, it's a shame you don't walk around. I mean, isn't this why people travel to other countries? You know, to see new places, different from where they come from." I looked at her, smiling and repeating her words in my mind, amazed how a path to a solution so often appears in an unexpected place. I will renovate a house that can't be found elsewhere, not even in London. I will recreate an old Tel Aviv apartment, entirely different from the ones seen in journals. I have had enough of open spaces, wooden floors, low couches, limited colours. I will find photos of old apartments and design a new one in their spirit.

When the lawyer called again I said: "I am willing to renovate your home only if you agree that I do something different. Not a modern design, but an old-fashioned one, in the spirit of Tel Aviv in mid-twentieth century." After a moment of silence he replied: "Abigail, my wife left me. I am rather depressed and I need a fresh start. Do whatever you want."

*

The prize committee asserted that the interior design of the apartment "is a perfect combination of old and new, history and future. It opens doors to local design and encouraged the connection between the spirit of a place and the nature of its homes. The perception of the past is both original and unique." Photos of the apartment were published in the International Journal of Design. The lawyer, who initially had been unhappy with the place, was so excited as the photographers came, as if he were the one who had won the prize. He called his friends, asking them to look for the photos in this prestigious journal of design. I simply stood there, observing how every detail was being photographed from various angles, wondering how it would look in the magazine.

My mother's response was rather surprising. When she found out about the prize, for a single moment her oppressive sadness completely disappeared; she cried with joy, hugged me and kissed my forehead. I don't recall ever seeing her so cheerful. She immediately called her friends, announcing the good news. She knew I had been working on a special project, but knew nothing of its nature. When I saw how happy she was I began to explain, elaborate on the fundamental novelty in the project. A revival of old Tel Aviv, buildings that connect with their surroundings, in a way it is a journey in time—she was thrilled, her eyes were wide open, she was so attentive she could hardly breathe. When I concluded she kissed me again and asked if it was possible to see the flat.

But when we left the place her mood was completely altered. After walking around quietly, almost on tiptoes, her face betraying amazement, while here and there she stretched her hand and touched a table or an old wooden cabinet, we drove home in complete silence. When we got there she sat in the big leather armchair facing the view, but it was obvious she saw nothing. The grey sea stretched to the horizon, and only a golden light lasting after sunset could be seen in the distance. Mum leaned her head against the headrest and closed her eyes. For a moment I was in panic. "Are you okay?"

"Yes. Wonderful work, Abigail."

"Then why are you sad?"

"I am not sad, I am immersed in my memories. This place resurrected old memories. Suddenly it felt as if it was the apartment we used to live in with Dad. Something about the colours was unbelievably familiar. It has been so many years, but I was reminded of our life there: friends coming over to dine, Dad addicted to work, determined and energetic. And then you were born. Everything was so different then. It's hard to explain, but back then the future was a central part of the present. Today people talk about how one should live in the moment; then people used to talk about the future, how to prepare for it, how to shape it."

"Yes, there is something depressing about this focus on the present. If you haven't enjoyed it, the moment is gone forever."

"True. And Dad was a person completely focused on the future. Always busy with plans, how to develop the business in ways no one else had thought of. He was a character, your father. Always directed at a single target, channelling all his capacities towards one aim. In fact, he never wanted to get married. Not because he didn't love me—he was crazy about me. But family made him divide his energies, and it was out of character, it went against the grain. He loved you madly but didn't want any more children. Fatherhood was stressful, and again it required splitting his attention. He used to explore one thing only. You know, you are very much like him. Gifted as he was, and directed at one purpose at a time."

A new, unfamiliar comfort formed, expanding and overflowing, filling me completely, like a deep breath of fresh air, creating a blush and bright eyes: I am like my dad, that's all. A couple of words can blur years of wondering why I am different, what went wrong with me. But now the explanation has been found, a justification that doesn't generate scepticism and despair but rather a pleasant path from the past to the present, and then to the future. The oppressive need that never quite disappears—that someone would determine that I am normal, that my being different would be justified, my strange emotions would be found reasonable and legitimate—is now replaced by ease: it feels as though I have just been found innocent. I relaxed on the sofa, smiling to myself, so grateful for Mum's words. But she didn't seem to understand how comforting they were. Her eyes were closed and clearly she was going back to her memories, sometimes smiling, sometimes straight-faced. The sun had already set, the sea was black and stormy, and lights of a huge ship could be seen on the horizon.

As I put my hand on hers, she opened her eyes, and they were full of tears.

"Mum, thanks for saying that. You have no idea what it means to me."

She looked at me and wiped away the tears, her hand was slightly trembling and her face a bit limp. "Sometimes I wonder what would have happened if Dad were alive."

The absolution I have just been granted made me happy and generous, and I replied: "Apparently I would have realized how much we were alike. Come on Mum, let's celebrate my success. Would you like me to come with you tomorrow to meet your friends?"

*

What a relief that autumn is finally here—jogging along the beach is so pleasant now. The early morning air is clear and soft, the water rushes along. The waves don't hit the shore but slowly approach it and then quickly recede. Other joggers seem more relaxed. The end of the summer is dispiriting, and autumn always brings a sigh of relief.

The renovation of the building in Shenkin Street is finally over, though I find the result somewhat disappointing. Months of investigating electricity and water systems, supporting old walls and adding external layers, all this effort did not produce the expected result. Everyone is praising it, and so do I, but I know it isn't right. Something went wrong, but I am not quite sure what. The boss kept saying that the front should fit the new spirit of the street, in which coffee shops and restaurants are crowded throughout the day, but I think the result is too artificial and polished. It would have been enough simply to clean the exterior walls and paint them. Now they are too smooth, too modern, highlighting the poor condition of the surrounding neighbourhood and the old and shabby houses.

But the boss is very pleased. This project, so he believes, will promote the firm, and bring more clients looking for large-scale renovations, perhaps even with some historical significance. The municipality of Tel Aviv may even consider us when it is planning some new projects—maybe other municipalities as well. He organized an event, invited journalists who took endless pictures of the building, and elaborated time and again on "the concept of our work."

I am not sure why, but I invited my father. I may have wanted to boast about the attention my work is getting, or perhaps I thought, unconsciously, that he would agree that the building isn't right for this street. Anyway, I decided to invite him. I was slightly afraid he would make tasteless jokes with all the young women. He showed up wearing an elegant suit, patted me on the back, and examined the building with great interest. At once I saw there was something different about his expression, but I was distracted but the crowd: camera flashes, speeches, people walking around with thin, long-stemmed wine glasses, I didn't think it meant anything. He moved around the place, stopping next to me once in a while, politely joining the conversation. As I was standing next to the boss he suddenly showed up, introduced himself and said how proud of me he was. The boss asked him what he did and he answered in detail, describing his business, emphasizing what he thought the boss might find useful.

I watched him, perplexed. The dignified appearance, the hair combed back, created a spiritual expression, so different from his usual ridiculous winking and vulgar sniggers. Also he was using high language, without any slang. It was clear the boss was impressed by him. He inquired about some details and posed questions suggesting a possible future professional connection. As they were talking my father suddenly interrupted the conversation, shook the boss's hand, thanked him and walked away. He didn't stare openly at young women in his normal manner and spoke very little, maintaining a dignified silence as he walked around. I followed him curiously.

When we left an unusual silence fell. A wind whistled between the houses, high clouds covered the sky, and street lamps shed soft light. The street was full of people, and we walked silently, immersed in our thoughts. I am not sure why but his unusual appearance made me nervous. There was something unfamiliar about him, an obscure refinement, so different from his usual vulgar masculinity. For a moment I thought perhaps he had been trying to establish a professional connection with the boss—but I knew I was wrong. His business was flourishing. I watched him out of the corner of my eye and I saw, yet again, the unexpected, thoughtful expression.

"Dad, are you okay? You look rather strange today. You're awfully quiet."

He stared at me and smiled.

"Come on, did something happen?"

He said nothing.

"Dad, you're scaring me. Say something. How is the renovation?"

"Nice."

"Nice? That's all?"

"Yes."

"Frankly, I also don't think the result is too impressive. The building in itself is nice, but it doesn't blend with the surroundings." He gave a short, shrill, laugh. "I knew you would agree. Everyone says how beautiful it is, but I know it isn't right."

He looked at me, distracted.

"Did you plan all of it?"

"With two other architects. And the boss inspected our plans."

"Which part did you plan?"

"Frankly, the front."

He smiled at himself, as if he had heard an amusing joke.

"If you had a chance, what would you change?"

"I honestly don't know. I don't understand what went wrong. It seemed like an excellent building plan, but it turned out to be wrong. I guess I would have designed the very same front again."

"The truth is that most people would repeat their mistakes. They are sorry, but they would do the very same thing again." His voice cracked. He didn't turn his head to me but stared into the distance. His grey hair blowing in the wind looked like a halo around his head. Street lamps shed orange light on his face. An old fear was awakened, a worm that slowly slithers forward.

"What do you mean?"

"I don't know, that's how I feel. I would certainly repeat my own mistakes."

"What mistakes?"

The worm contracted and stretched and moved forward.

A boy in bed pretending to be asleep, listening to voices behind the closed door, anxious that Dad would leave.

"I wasn't a good father. I should have taken better care of you. But I'm afraid I would do exactly the same again."

"It's a consequence of the divorce, isn't it? It's hard to be a good father without living at home."

"Yes, that's part of it, no doubt."

"Frankly I don't understand why the two of you ever got married. You are such different people."

He didn't answer. The worm of fear was burrowing inside me. The weeping I've heard years ago, Mum crying quietly. As I get out of bed and hug her she swallows the tears and wipes her nose, embracing me and saying nothing. What will happen now?

Dad stopped walking. The left side of his face was visible, the right side was dark. I don't think I had ever seen him like this.

"I am very glad you invited me to this event. Really, it means a lot to me."

"Okay. I didn't know it was so important. Another event, that's all."

"It matters to me—you inviting me to celebrate your project."

He turned, his eyes were a little shiny. In seconds of silence the worm bit me, maybe at the heart, maybe somewhere else, hurting me, and it kept slithering on: please, not a new, unfamiliar story, I can't take it, not blaming Mum, attacking her. Leave our life story the way I know it.

"I am sorry, but not the way you think. I regret letting insults affect me. You pushed me away, never wanted me around. Until recently you would never let me present myself as your father, not in parents' conferences, in school gatherings, making sure that I would never say I'm Guy's father. Children don't understand that, but parents are insulted and driven away."

"It's hardly my fault."

"Everything between children and their parents is first of all the parents' fault. But I let it get to me. I should have ignored it, acted as if I haven't heard it. But had I been given the chance, I would probably do the same thing again."

"Dad, you left us."

"I didn't have a choice."

The worm is moving again, digging an oppressive and painful tunnel. Mum throws his clothes to the trash, her face pale, and she moves nervously. I stand there watching her, wondering if she would put my stuff in the trash too.

"Why?"

"I never concealed who I am and the way I live. Not even from your mother. She knew who she was marrying. But I thought she could live with it, maybe enjoy the company of other men. But when I saw how depressed she was I decided it would be better to divorce."

"Why did you marry her in the first place?"

"Your mother was in love with me and I wanted to be a father. I suppose I wanted it because that's how you leave something behind after you're dead, your blood living on through your children. I have five children from three women, and I thank God for that. And your mother got over it too. She's been living with Joel for years now. But I should have taken better care of you, and ignored these stupid insults."

The worm had expanded so much that it was too big to burrow within me, a painful bulk that quickly transforms fear into repressed anger.

"That's why you wanted children?"

"Yes."

"Not to love them? To raise them?"

"I love each one of you very much. As I have said, I should have taken better care of you."

Heartbeats. The worm cracked and disappeared. Sheer confidence had taken it place: I will never be like him, ever, I don't care if I leave something behind me in this world. A child is not a means but an end. I have had enough of this functional point of view, everything serves a purpose. And I am untouched by his empty words on haunting insults and unfulfilled care. Fatherhood implies changing, making concessions. Dad wasn't willing to do this. His words couldn't mask that.

A sudden gust of wind hit us. We bowed our backs against it and began to walk slowly. I looked at him and saw his eyes were moist, for a moment his face betrayed a self-indulgent expression of disappointment mixed with sorrow, but he quickly adopted a practical tone.

"Now that you and Abigail have broken up, are you dating other women?"

"Yes. Not many."

"Is there someone you like?"

"Each one reminds me how I miss her."

"Did you discuss it with anyone?"

"With Daphne. She thought that, if this is how I feel, perhaps I should try to make Abigail change her mind. Strange, we ran into each other coincidentally in the centre of Tel Aviv, and had a very long discussion on true love, children, parenthood."

"And how does Amir feel about it?"

"No idea. I told him about the chance encounter with

Daphne. The only thing that he wanted to know was if we met on Basel Street, at what time, and what was she doing there."

Eighteenth Month

So this is what the bed looks like after sex with a stranger: a head turned aside with only the brown of the hair visible, two round breasts, below them a straight line of a beige blanket, red hair perpendicular to it. A masculine arm bent at a right angle. Our legs creating waves in the blanket that slips to the side of the bed, and forms a soft, shiny triangle. The only thing spoiling the geometrical mosaic of the room is the half-folded burgundy rug by the bed.

Jonathan looks away, perhaps to conceal his disappointment. This is not how he wished this date to end. This is the third time we've met. Each time, in the afternoon, at his house. I left Tomer with my mother and lied about having a dentist appointment. Jonathan kept calling me after we ran into each other, imploring me to meet. Eventually I agreed. Frankly, from the very first call I knew I would agree, only a ridiculous pretence stopped me from accepting the invitation after the first call. A sort of coquetry, as if it was appropriate to hesitate, refuse, and then give in. But I knew all along what was about to take place.

He wanted a relationship that would leave a beautiful memory; I wanted to experience lust born of alienation. His desire was refined; I wished to see my body through yearning eyes. He was hoping to complete some unfinished business; I was trying to cure some mental weakness that has been part of me since I gave birth. Each time we met my weakness became more evident, the constant self-doubt, the inner looseness, something that was previously tightly secured is now cracked, and the parts don't fall into place properly.

The first time I went to his place there was a touch of uncertainty. Autumn wind swayed the trees facing the balcony, dry leaves fluttered in the air, and a flock of birds sat on an electric wire in front of the building. His face betrayed deep excitement as he began touching me, but I ignored it, indicating physical pleasure and nothing more. A masculine hand caressing smooth skin, a long body on top of round curves, every passing moment made the woman in the bed prettier. Our second date, a month later, took place on a bright cloudless winter day. A whimsical spirit overtook us, as if we were two children getting into mischief. Jonathan made fun of the flowered pattern on my lingerie, exhibiting odd and quirky knowledge of women's underwear. As he unhooked my bra he mumbled, "Uh... good quality" and I burst out laughing. But now he is serious. He had the countenance of someone who is about to say something, but is too timid. His brows were furrowed and looked determined, and then he changed his mind.

I have no interest in his confessions. I don't want to blur our being strangers, to pretend that an intimacy has been created. On the contrary, I enjoy the distance. The feeling of adventure wouldn't have lasted if we became friends. After every date I am high-spirited, but this mood fades after a couple of days. Though I am better dressed now, even when I take Tomer for a walk or go shopping. I placed the pregnancy dresses and some shabby pants and shirts in the bottom drawer, and I am wearing my pre-pregnancy clothes. When I take a walk with Tomer I sometimes purchase a shirt or a dress. But when I look in the mirror a couple of days after meeting Jonathan, again a young woman who has aged a little is facing me, curvy in some obscure way, and in her eyes I see a mixture of happiness and despair.

Amir's wariness makes this adventure even more delightful. I don't know what raised his suspicions, I was very careful not to reveal anything, but jealousy makes him such a nice husband. He offers to wash the dishes, insists I must take a rest, suggests we go to the coffee shop in the evening. Every time my phone rings he asks in a casual manner who it is; this charade almost makes me laugh. He also calls a couple of times during the morning, asking where I am, if I am "having a good time". Odd that such an intelligent man behaves in such a ludicrous manner, as though inquiring would stop me from betraying him. But still, a rod twisted and bent since I became pregnant is gradually straightening, resuming its original shape. An obscure mechanism is working properly again, according to its inner logic, connecting us in a natural and desirable manner. He no longer treats my body as if it were made of glass but reveals a more determined aspect of himself, normally unseen. He seems like a quiet and indecisive man, but the truth is he is very stubborn.

Jonathan calls me "a beauty", Amir says I am "attractive"; Jonathan suggests we find an excuse and take a one-day trip; Amir suggests we spend a night in a hotel. I find the attention flattering, I am happy for a couple of hours, but then the looseness takes over again.

I feel as if I had already used most of my strength, and must now be careful not to waste any effort, to avoid exhaustion.

My actions are always preceded by a latent calculation, never fully conscious, an invisible scale that has weakness, pain, the delivery on one side and motherhood on the other. And their complements change nothing; they never ever tip the scale and they never engender a spirit of rejuvenation.

Only Tomer makes me sigh with relief. When he crawls away from me as fast as he can and then looks back at me as if caught in mischief, staring at me smiling, when he bursts into laughter, I feel that the ancient musical instrument within me finally makes a new, pleasant sound, and not a dreary old one.

"Come here, you naughty boy," I call him, pretending to chase him.

He tries to crawl as fast as he can but this interferes with his hand and leg coordination and he falls forwards, chuckling joyfully. I pick him up and sit him on my lap, his big eyes sparkle with happiness, his four tiny teeth, two in the upper jaw and two in the lower, are visible when he laughs, making him look like a baby animal and not a toddler, and the downy red hair covering his head emphasizes the soft milky skin. He hugs me tightly, his head fits perfectly into the rounded space between my chest, neck and head.

We sit on the carpet and he puts blocks into a big box. First the green ones, then red, yellow, blue. His face is so serious, engrossed in this difficult operation. He moves his hands with full concentration, careful not to drop a single block out of the box. Suddenly I see he looks exactly like Amir: strain makes him furrow his brow and tighten his mouth, he is fully absorbed in a task and determined to complete it. Aaron once told me that when Amir was a baby he would never let go of a toy until all the parts were in place, even if he was very hungry. Tired and exhausted, Aaron would place a bottle right in front of him, but he never touched it until the block tower was tall and stable. Tomer is stubborn like his father, crawling to the farthest block, holding it and struggling to crawl back with it, then as he puts it in the box he smiles at me in triumph. Yet, unlike his father, when all the blocks are in place he gladly kicks the box and it falls over, the blocks are spread on the carpet, and he erupts into loud joyful laughter. In spite of his effort, he has no desire to cling to achievement; like me, he is indifferent to success, kicking the box and starting all over again, dividing the blocks by colour and putting them one after another into the box.

Then we have lunch. I put sliced vegetables on his plate, he bites them with his four teeth, nibbling and sucking until all that is left are tiny red and green pieces. He takes each one and cautiously puts it in his mouth. Then comes the hot dish, a purée of potatoes and meat. He opens his mouth wide, waiting for the spoon to sink into the bowl, lift up full of food, and quickly enter his mouth without the meat falling out. When the spoon is empty and returns to the bowl he opens his mouth again, slamming his fists on the tray before him, demanding to have his hunger satisfied. After he has had a couple of spoons I place the bowl before him, letting him try to eat on his own. First he grabs the spoon and tries to dip it in the bowl. As he realizes that he is unable to do this he puts down the spoon and grabs the purée with his hand and brings it to its mouth. His round face is smeared with food: cheeks, nose, chin, even the neck. Time and again he tries to put food in his mouth, smiling at me. As he sees that I am grinning he figures there must be some charm in food smeared all over him. He then stretches out a chubby hand, takes some purée and tosses it happily on the floor, watching it drop, laughing with such joy...

I look at him and for a moment I am breathless. In a

minute I will join him and throw food on the floor, giggle at the sight of tiny pieces of meat splashing all over. His chuckle is so sweet and inviting, the pleasure of permissiveness is so rich, this game is such fun. Tomer and I will compete over who can throw the food the farthest. His eyes are ecstatically bright, his smile is mischievous and captivating as he says *mamamamama* and I hear Mummy, Mummy; his bliss is enchanting and I want to intensify it, to share in it. His freedom is so full and uninhibited—why confine him, why prevent this unbridled satisfaction?

Tomer is so excited, he grabs the bowl and is about to throw it as well. In a minute the floor will be covered with small pieces of food and the sound of his rolling laughter will fill the kitchen. "No, Tomer, you can't do that," a voice is emerging from within me, startlingly similar to my mother's. Bewildered, he looks at me, wondering why I should change my mind all of a sudden and reproach him in such a harsh tone. I hold the bowl and he slowly lets go of it, not laughing any more but watching me, almost crying.

I am so sorry, sadness overwhelms me, these shrill tones almost bring tears to my eyes. Love and devotion are not enough, discipline is unavoidable; and it makes me angry and increases my weakness. I gradually withdraw into myself, wipe purée off the table, place the dirty plates in the sink, lift Tomer and cuddle him, as he sobs bitterly and hits me with his small hand.

When he falls asleep in my lap I carry him carefully to bed. I stand by the bed, softly wiping his tears, eager to ask for forgiveness, but he is fast asleep, indifferent to my sadness. It will all be forgotten tomorrow, I tell myself, immediately dismissing my own words.

*

I will kill him. I don't care. I will kill him. When I find out who he is I'll make sure he disappears. I will hire a private detective. Or I'll follow Daphne myself and find out who she's having an affair with.

Better not. I don't think I will be able to see her with another man (I might faint). The mere thought of a strange hand touching the long and curved body, the breasts that are fuller now, the long red hair falling on her light-skinned back chills me. This new glamour of hers scares me: the back is straighter now, the makeup bolder, and there is a certain freedom of movement. Even the palms of her hands (which are normally slightly rough) now seem strong and smooth, and the finger joints flexible and pretty.

I better not see them together. If I do, I'll never be able to erase the memory.

Maybe I'll tell Guy about it and ask him what to do. No, I don't want him to know. It would establish his superiority again, which has gradually faded through the years. When he told me that he and Abigail had broken up he seemed so distressed, his face betraying a panic I had never seen before—it almost pleased me. If I tell him Daphne is cheating on me he will have this "expert on women" tone. I don't need this now.

Maybe I'll talk to my father. His compassion is always so comforting. I will ask him what to do. (On second thoughts, I better not.)

Who could it be? Who could she meet now? She spends all her time with Tomer. Maybe Ron, her ex-boyfriend? Perhaps he decided to look for her? Maybe someone she knew in school? In college?

(This smile of hers, the huge eyes are so bright, you can just tell.)

Since she hung up the phone as she saw me enter the room I became suspicious. Suddenly it hit me, the phone rings and she often disconnects without answering. But this time she blushed and murmured something about an advertising call. I then realized that what I thought was recovery from pregnancy was really a different feminine bloom, sensual and arousing. The peach tone lipstick she always has on her lips, the shining long hair, the flattering dresses, my unanswered calls (she then claims she never heard the phone ringing), all those details suddenly created a clear picture, with sharp strident colours. The fear that came with this moment of insight made me furious. I accused Daphne of not taking proper care of Tomer, he was hungry and she wasn't preparing food. She looked at me astounded, her big eyes wide, but said nothing. And I kept arguing and explaining, my heart shivering with horror and pain.

Jealousy is strange. It creates such conflicting reactions. One moment I am about to explode with terrible anger, the next I am contemplating carefully what I should do. In a minute I'll push Daphne against the wall and demand that she tells me if she is cheating on me and with whom, and immediately afterwards I act with kindness, eager to appear as caring and considerate as possible. Whenever I think about it I swing between an impulse to scream, to blame, to take revenge—and a natural instinct not to let the invisible opponent win. I have never experienced such envy. I used to be jealous of Guy's success with women, and my admitted failure created only sadness, but here there is no room for gloom. My suspicion of Daphne's infidelity is oppressive and exhausting, and it doesn't disappear for a single moment.

A thought crossed my mind, I could tell her about Sari. I immediately decided against it. I was sitting in my office in the evening, pondering whether I should go home and spend time with Tomer, or stay and avoid this suffocating envy. The phone rang. Sari. In her provocative tone she inquired if I would like "to come tomorrow at noon," and then added that she could only stay at home for half an hour, forty-five minutes at most. Silence. I didn't answer. I closed my eyes and said nothing. Sari was astonished, she didn't understand what was happening; why was I not asking her when exactly I should be there? After a few moments of silence, she asked: "Amir, can you hear me?"

"Yes."

"So why don't you answer me?"

"…"

"Amir?"

"You won't see me again. Ever."

"Ah, poodle, is this another one of your resolutions?"

"I won't be coming to see you anymore."

I disconnected. My breathing could be heard in the silent room, sharp and fast. The spider web that attached me to her (oppressive, vile, but holding me fast) was torn in an instant. I have been trying to break away from her for months, and all of a sudden I realized I didn't want to see her any more. Her mysterious smile conceals nothing but vulgarity, the sin provokes nothing but shame, and my self-disgust becomes a drug I need more and more.

But they all disappeared in a flash. From the moment I

realized Daphne was having an affair Sari turned into a shell that I am about to shed. No longer is she a sensual woman who makes Daphne look a bit dull, now she is the mirror reflecting Daphne's light: her gaze is never dreamy, her full body never evokes longing but only lust, her giggle as I leave her lacks softness, and her condescending tone emphasizes Daphne's good heart. Strange how I knew on the spot that the affair with Sari was over; a slight feeling of relief slipped in alongside the depressing jealousy.

The phone is ringing again. Sari. I look at it, wondering what to do, should I take revenge for her insults, or let go. I close my eyes, a ring, another one, another one, then silence. It is ringing again, ten rings, eleven, and at the twelfth ring it stops. My head leaning back, my eyes closed, my hands clinging to the armrests, I am saved, I can't believe it, I am saved, I didn't fall into the abyss! Its edge is so tempting but at the bottom there is a sodden swamp.

I sat motionless, giving in to the new sensation as I tried to understand it, but I couldn't figure out what was happening. I am saved, I said to myself, saved (wondering why I am feeling so uneasy). Piles of papers covered my desk, the computer screen was full of numbers, various receipts were placed in the box on my right, Tomer's picture was facing me – it all looked the same. Everything appears unchanged. Still I wondered why I felt as though some hidden order had secretly been disrupted. Only after long minutes of sitting still with eyes closed did it occur to me that perhaps an inner pattern was stretching and assuming a new shape, alien and unfamiliar.

I imagined Daphne's naked body, her face when she is excited, and suddenly I saw a new quality blending with my lust, something I didn't quite understand. A new sense interlaced with my desire, transforming its nature into something I didn't quite understand.

You chicken, I said to myself, jealousy has made you an even bigger coward than usual. Why don't you confront her, ask her in an assertive way with whom she is having an affair, then act indifferent, that's what you should do. I will teach her a lesson, she can't deceive me like this, I will tell her about Sari, about our encounters. I'll make her so sorry she ever cheated on me.

It's useless, the words were meagre and empty. I tried to think of Sari, to picture some passionate moments, but a part of me has fallen away and has ceased to exist, and I was not sure what had replaced it. Horror filled me as I realized that my crude lust has disappeared along with my affair with Sari; I thought anxiously that my masculinity was somehow flawed.

I didn't know what was happening to me. Was it all the result of my jealousy? Of being a father?

When I have a chance I will speak to my father about it.

Nineteenth Month

"Mum, what's this portfolio case doing here?"

"Ah, nothing really. Where is my sweet grandson?"

"He caught cold and stayed at home with Daphne. What's this portfolio case doing here?"

"Amiri, it's really nothing…"

"Mum!"

"Oh, very well, I'll tell you. I've started painting."

"What? You started what?"

"Painting."

"You? Painting? I find that hard to believe. You were never interested in art."

"I was busy with other things."

"When did you start?"

"Three months ago. I saw an ad for an art course and decided to give it a go."

"But you can't paint. Sorry Mum, no offence, I meant that you never did any drawing before."

"True. When I called the teacher I told her I haven't used colours since I was a child. She asked why I decided to try now. I said three months ago I became a grandma, and suddenly I am eager to try new things. She replied that she couldn't think of a better reason."

"So what happened?"

"Well, I was terribly embarrassed in the first class. Everyone began working and I had no idea what I should do. I could hardly make a couple of lines. But the teacher explained about proportions and I gradually made some progress. Frankly I don't care that much what my paintings look like—the point is I'm enjoying it so much."

"What do you paint?"

"Sometimes there is a model in class, sometime we go outdoors and draw open landscape, or interesting buildings."

"Amazing. I'm speechless. That's the last thing in the world I would think of you doing."

"I'm just as surprised as you really, but, you know, the need to experience new things runs very deep."

"Can I see the pictures?"

"I'd rather you didn't. They are hardly masterpieces..."

"Please, can I? It's very interesting."

"Oh, well, whatever..."

"Did you make that?"

"Yes."

"Impossible."

"..."

"Surely the teacher assisted you?"

"No, I made this one two weeks ago."

"I can't believe it. Are you sure you made it all by yourself?"

"Yes."

"Wow... You're so gifted!"

"Thanks."

"Keep doing this, Mum, these pictures are wonderful!"

"Thanks, Amiri. Well, class starts in half an hour, so I should be on my way. Dad is watching TV in the study. He didn't hear you come in. Kiss my adorable grandson."

"Of course. See you."

*

"Dad, I didn't know Mum could paint so well."

"I know. Me neither. She never even told me she was taking lessons. A couple of weeks ago I came home early and found her arranging the pictures."

"Weird, I never would have imagined she would take an art course."

"Tomer's coming into the world did her so much good. She almost turned into a different person. Suddenly she is vital in a way I haven't seen for years. No doubt for her Tomer's birth was a closure. Something that has been a burden for years, perhaps she wasn't even aware how oppressive it was, is gone. Interesting how the birth of a child can have such an effect."

"Not everyone is affected in such a positive way."

"What do you mean?"

"I don't know. It's hard to explain."

"Tomer is such a wonderful boy. You are very fortunate."

"I know, he is amazing. I find myself missing him when I am at work. Still—"

"Son, what is the problem?"

"It's complicated."

"Has to do with women?"

"Yes. Sort of."

"What do you mean by 'sort of'?"

"Remember I was having an affair? Not that I'm proud of it, in fact quite the opposite, I'm ashamed. But it ended strangely."

"'Strangely'?"

161

"All of a sudden I didn't want to see her at all."

"Guilt?"

"No, not at all. As I've said, I'm ashamed of myself, but that's not quite the issue. I don't know how to put this... Dad, I suspect that Daphne is cheating on me. I am not quite sure, it may all be in my head, but the moment I became suspicious I completely lost interest in that other woman."

"I find it hard to believe that Daphne is betraying you. A young woman who just had her first child, I don't think so."

"I am not quite sure, but that's still not the problem."

"Are you sorry for this woman?"

"Not at all. Frankly, I don't like her at all. The thing is... it is hard to say this. I think this affair has changed me, and it scares me."

"How did it change you?"

"Well, you know men have two types of passion for women, one plain and bestial, the other more refined? I don't know how to say this, but I think I've lost the first one. And it is terrifying."

"Listen, Amiri, becoming a parent is a huge change, which often isn't acknowledged enough. A person sees himself in a new light, and it stirs up all sorts of emotions. I am not sure that a year from today you will feel the same. People adjust gradually."

"Did you feel this way when I was born?"

"For us, you know, everything went wrong. Overnight I became both a father and a mother. The truth is I had no choice, but I remember wondering if your mum and I could ever... Amiri, this is too embarrassing."

"Sorry. I didn't mean to inquire about the details, only about your feelings."

"I think parenthood somehow shifts the centre of gravity,

and this affects everything: daily routine, work, relationship between partners, and apparently also one's self-perception."

"Don't be offended by my question, but, but, is this the beginning of old age?"

"Why should I be offended? No. I don't think it is the beginning of old age but the end of youth. Probably that's what is bothering you."

"I never was an adventurous adolescent."

"True, but there is always the illusion that it is still possible, that it could happen. Now you say to yourself you will never ever have this liberated youth again, and you are afraid of disillusion. By the way, in my opinion there is nothing frightening about it."

"About what? Disillusion?"

"Yes, because it is followed by tranquillity. Accepting what one doesn't have leads to enjoyment of what one does have. And you have so much: a wonderful son, a good wife, a new family, a future. There is no need to cling to youth, Amiri; it will be over anyway. What is important is that what follows it is good and right."

"Yes, but the experience of youth has an impact even when it is gone."

"People often feel this way. I am not at all sure it's true. I was very shy when I was younger, and I knew very few women before I met your mom. Still, I have always considered myself fortunate for marrying her and having a family. I was very sorry for the suffering that the delivery brought, for many reasons, one of which is that we wanted a big family, and after your birth it was clear that it was impossible."

"I don't know, Dad. They were different times. People had different expectations."

"Yes, that's probably true. Still, it is better to focus on the future and not on the past."

"I am concerned about the future."

"You know, Amir, I think you should make a change; but not the way you think."

"What do you mean?"

"You should spend more time with Tomer, take part in raising him. You're missing a wonderful thing, and you'll be sorry for that. I know you work hard, but still, I think it's possible."

"I am pretty sure that the boss wants to promote me, and I am the sole earner right now."

"Daphne needs to go back to work and you need to spend more time at home. I'm certain that this is the right thing for the both of you."

Twentieth Month

This morning, standing behind the closed door, I couldn't make up my mind if I should stay or leave. I heard Tomer sobbing on the other side of the door, panicked and enraged, almost choking. I stopped myself from leaning against the door and weeping. In a moment I would have stretched out my hand and opened the door, lifted him into my arms, kissed him and mumbled: "Mummy isn't leaving you," and hurried away with him.

Two days ago I returned to work at the social welfare office. Gal and Rotem greeted me with such open joy, they even placed a pot of violets on my desk. Amid computer screens, files and forms, the purple flowers in a bright green flowerpot were startling. A piece of blooming nature planted in this sombre office drowning in heart-breaking stories. Even the Aunties greeted me gladly, asking about Tomer, how I am doing, who is looking after him. I've found a good nanny, I said, she has very good recommendations, a very nice woman, no, he is not by himself, there are two other toddlers—I kept wondering if he was still leaning against the door, crying and begging me to take him out of this place.

As we were having dinner, about a month ago, Amir

raised the question whether I should go back to work. In a slightly apologetic tone he wondered if we should look for a nanny, maybe it was "about time" to find a place where Tomer could stay during the day. He was feeding him dinner as he said this, smiling, attempting to conceal his embarrassment and a hint of accusation. When I said nothing he went on: Tomer is already more than ten months old, it's about time to look for a nanny. He understands I didn't want to leave him when my maternity leave was over, but now he feels it is the right thing to do. Tomer is very friendly, he is always watching other children and smiling at them. He is sure that after a period of adjustment he would be very happy. And also, I would be able to return to the social welfare office. He knows how much I love that place. And if I don't return soon, someone may take my place.

Tomer, now already eating by himself, grabbed a spoon and deliberately dropped it on the floor. He thoroughly enjoyed this, though he knew it was not allowed. The spoon's falling would be followed by reproachful words, but then it would be given back to him, and he could throw it once again. This time Amir did not rebuke him but picked up the spoon silently and placed it on the table. Tomer looked at him surprised, perhaps even disappointed, wondering why his father isn't explaining time and again that he can't throw utensils on the floor. The magic of the game was almost gone: without the reproach there is no pleasure in ignoring it, and tossing the spoon is almost pointless. Yet not only did Amir say nothing, he even smiled at him and caressed his head softly. He cleaned Tomer's face with a wipe and said, "After you take a bath, Daddy will tell you a story."

I said nothing. Some things cannot simply be uttered in conversation; the weakness, the fear of leaving Tomer with a stranger, the distress of knowing how he would suffer. The truth is, I thought, that I am anxious that life will return to its old routine, the way it was before Tomer was born. Not that it wasn't a good life, on the contrary, I often thought how fortunate I was. But now I'm afraid of falling back into the former routine, as if it would spoil the happiness of Tomer's coming into this world and blur the fragility it created.

Amir said he feels it would be better for me, and he was positive that if I don't return to work, eventually I would feel I had missed something, especially since I love this job so much. Tomer was silent, gazing first at Amir and then at me, as if he could understand what we were saying. He put down the spoon and stopped eating, watching us like a judge. And I felt that once the words about returning to work had been articulated, there was no way of taking them back. There was no way to discuss it, question, hesitate—that is what everyone does, these days parents don't stay at home with their children but rather go back to work. Trying to find another solution would necessarily be seen as an attempt to avoid sharing the burden, dodging responsibility.

"Daphne, you look so sad," Amir said, stroking my hair and embracing me. Lately his jealously had assumed a new, softer shape. His face no longer betrayed a suppressed anger, as he offered help. Now it was replaced by an unfamiliar tenderness, compassion tinged with sadness. When he comes home he holds Tomer with one arm and hugs me with the other, keeping us both close to his body as if we were two halves of one entity. Sometimes he even smiles and says: "Here is my family", embarrassed and blushing but insisting on showing his affection. Tomer is cheerful, and I am tranquil in his arms, surrendering to his warmth. Finally each one of us takes one step back, and Amir carries Tomer to his toys.

A couple of days after we had this conversation I began to inquire about nannies. Without me asking for it, my mother suggested to look for someone "with very good recommendations." Gal called several times to find out when I was coming back to work. Even the head of the welfare office approached me, saying she wouldn't be able to keep my post for more than a year. Amir's parents offered to help the nanny. And so the decision that I would go back to work became almost unquestionable. Everyone began asking friends, inquiring about possible nannies, until, eventually, two weeks ago, I was facing Naomi's house, an elderly lady living by herself, looking after two toddlers. I rang the bell. As she opened the door I saw the two boys, a bit older than Tomer, looking at me with disappointment; they must have thought that I was their parents, coming to fetch them. Naomi was a full figured woman, walking slowly and heavily, in a darkened room full of cooking smells. In a low, quiet voice she described the daily routine of the toddlers, saying time and again how fastidious she was: she changed diapers without delay, removed dirty clothes on the spot, washed the blanket on the floor and disinfected the crockery every single day. While we were talking the two boys looked at us in bewilderment; one stood by the coffee table, grabbing it so as not to fall, examining me curiously; the other sat on the carpet, putting down the toy car and repeating in a sad voice, "Mummy, Mummy".

The windows did not allow any sunshine in. The very few toys packed in a small box, the worn-out furniture and dark carpet, the shabbiness more apparent because it was so clean—I knew on the spot that I would never leave Tomer there, but I pretended I was considering it. As I ran down the stairs, eager to get away from Naomi's house, I could somehow feel the heavy odour of soup. Amir listened patiently to my description of the place and then suggested we find someone who would watch Tomer at home.

Sometime later I opened the door to a tall, thin woman, about forty years old, smiling from ear to ear, taking off her jacket and immediately saying, "First of all, I want to see the sweet boy." Daniela had many references. She suggested we call the parents who gave them: "The best thing to do is to actually talk to the parents, that's how I feel. No matter what the letter says, one must ask the parents directly." Every couple of moments a broad smile would spread on her face, revealing large white teeth; then it would disappear in an instant. When Tomer approached her, walking slowly around the coffee table, holding on to it as not to fall, she took out of her purse a stuffed puppy, and made a sort of barking sound. He was thrilled and cried out loud: "_og, _og." Tomer's fine red hair has already turned into shiny curls, his body has become stronger, his posture more balanced. He smiled at the visitor, who was determined to make him express his joy. Daniela exuded nothing but confidence and authority, and every now and then she added, "I believe this is the proper way to treat a toddler." Finally she got up, brushing away from her clothes the crumbs of the cake I had served her, and reached for the stuffed puppy in Tomer's hand. He watched her in surprise, gradually letting go of the dog. She then exposed her white teeth again and said: "Next time I come I will bring it with me. Say 'bye' to Max," moving the stuffed dog as though it was saying goodbye. Tomer waved at her, and she smiled again and closed the door behind her.

Amir thought she was lovely. My mother looked into her references. Everyone said she was wonderful, in spite of some minor reservations: *she is often on the phone, once in a while she missed work, once a child was found crying in bed and she ignored her.* But all in all everyone thought she is a very good nanny. My mother insisted that she seems very reliable, and this is the most important thing. But I thought of her eyes examining the house meticulously, trying to assess if she would have to clean it, the empty cliché of "sweet boy," and the slightly husky voice that betrayed a very practical spirit that she was eager to conceal. "Daphne, she really looks okay," my mother said, "a nice, responsible nanny, with excellent recommendations, why don't you hire her? We are fortunate that she is available now, if you wait too long someone else would hire her." Amir kept saying we should take her. He thinks that the most important thing is experience, and clearly she is an accomplished nanny.

All these observations only annoyed me.

I found it strange that they didn't see her faults, and pretended not to notice how shrewd she is. The pressure to convince me to hire her on the spot made me angry. I insulted my mother by saying we would make the decision and not her, and annoyed Amir by murmuring that only I knew what was right for Tomer. But beneath the anger, a motherly instinct was awakening, an independent certainty, an ancient voice, soft yet constant, one that can be heard only when listening carefully, driving a mother to stretch out her hands before the child trips and falls, or fend off a threat in a friendly disguise. Her accelerated heartbeats conceal secrets that a casual glance would fail to observe.

I watched Tomer sitting on the rug, examining a children's book, pushing buttons making animal sounds. Every time a cow's moo or a rooster's crow was heard he looked at the book bemused and then turned to gaze at me, waiting for me to join in his astonishment that these huge animals hid in between the pages. Red curls covered his head and neck, the arms carried a roundness that the body was beginning to lose, the huge, curious eyes waited for me either to remove the invisible creatures or to explain how they inhabited the soft, plastic pages—like a cub clinging to his mother, afraid of wild animals—I turned to Amir and said with utter confidence: "I simply don't want this nanny. She is not right for him, that's all. I will find someone else."

Ruhama, a thin woman with black curly hair, and her lumpish, slow-walking husband lived in a one-story house between tall buildings. They looked after two toddlers. I came a bit early, and to my great surprise tears were running down her face as she opened the door. She apologized, "Sorry, forgive me, today is my late son's birthday, he died in a car accident. He would have been thirty-eight today. Never mind, in the afternoon his daughters are coming, and together we'll commemorate his birthday. They returned from France after the accident. Sorry, I didn't expect you so early. I was about to wash my face. Don't think I am always like this, it's a happy home, only today is a difficult day." She disappeared for a couple of minutes and then returned well dressed and made up. She described the daily routine of the toddlers, and when she was done I asked when we could start.

The first two days went well. When I first left Tomer in Ruhama's arms he looked surprised and even smiled, as if it was part of a game and soon I would appear from around the corner crying "peek-a-boo!" I drove slowly to the social welfare office, experiencing again, after long months, the transformation from the northern part of Tel Aviv, full of greenery, to the south of the city, now full of mud and puddles. I thought I would have the opportunity to readjust slowly to our office; I had forgotten the urgency, the crying and begging that so often filled it. After making conversation with the Aunties, and before I had a chance to put my purse in the lower drawer, a full figured woman was facing me. Her legs and feet, covered in bandages, were so swollen they hardly fit in her shoes. She collapsed into the chair, breathing heavily. She had come to me for help because her daughter, a single mother, was sick with pneumonia. Her granddaughter was only four, but she was disabled and was already too heavy for her grandmother to lift. They both love her dearly, but could I possibly send someone to help them until her daughter recovers?

This unassuming spirit, the utter acceptance of fate, was overwhelming. "She has a handicapped child," and not another word. She took a white handkerchief out of her purse and wiped the sweat off her face, and then folded it carefully and placed it back in her bag. Her full face, the protruding stomach under the black dress made of thick fabric, the swollen legs that looked like rolls of thick fabric, she didn't seem sad or desperate, only eager to help her daughter in any possible way. For a moment I imagined Tomer's plump legs, moving carefully as he edges around the coffee table, taking one step at a time, holding on to the table so as not to lose his balance, standing on tiptoes as if it were easier to walk forward like that.

"You see, my granddaughter has to be moved from the bed to the wheelchair," she kept explaining, shifting my attention at once from Tomer to the disabled girl. I am not sure why, but I began asking about her illness, though it was not at all necessary. She was born disabled, a lack of oxygen during labour affected her motor skills. "She's fine in the head, a smart girl," but she can't walk. Her mother insisted on sending her to a normal nursery school, so that she wouldn't see herself as sick, but now, when she herself is ill, she's unable to lift her.

The father? "Drinking problems, I'm glad he's gone." She kept describing their lives in detail, as though she were talking about another family and not her own. Strange that she isn't crying, a thought passed, she described her granddaughter without suggesting in any way that it could have been different, that the girl could have been running around in the nursery school.

I called the emergency centre. In the coming days volunteers will come twice a day, as long as it is needed. She thanked me as she got up, struggling to lift her heavy body, said goodbye, and walked very slowly to the exit. As she was standing in the corridor I heard her asking where the elevator was, she can't walk down the steps, not even one floor.

Just as I was going to call Ruhama, a tall, thin man, about fifty years old, reeking of cigarettes, walked into the room. He looked around nervously, shifted a cigarette butt from his right hand to his left, pulled out a chair and sat down. Clearly he wasn't used to visiting welfare offices. His small eyes had a sceptical look, as though there was no point in coming here but he had no other choice. He looked at Rotem, Gal and me defiantly, brushing his hair back with his hand every now and then, his skin wrinkled and burned by a blazing sun.

"Miss, I would like you to find a job for my son. He is seventeen years old," he said in a loud voice, and immediately elaborated, before I had a chance to ask, that the son has spent the last two years in a state boarding school, but two months ago he was forced to leave. He is not quite sure why, maybe he got into a fight, maybe he was taking drugs, though he claims this isn't the reason. Now he wanders about aimlessly, doing nothing, and he is afraid he will find refuge in drugs and crime.

My social worker's instincts were awakened: always listen to what isn't said, to what is intentionally concealed, hardship that leads to theft is presented as exploitation, aggressiveness is portrayed as self-defence.

"May I ask why your son went to the state boarding school?" I asked.

He shifted the cigarette butt from hand to hand with an effort not to light it and replied, "We have four children. My wife and I work very hard, she is a cleaner and I work in construction. You see, it's very difficult to take care of the kids, we return home late at night. The three older ones did well, but it was very hard for the youngest, the one who needs a job. He got into trouble in school so we sent him to a state boarding school. We thought he'd be fine, that someone would look after him. But now he got into trouble again, and was kicked out. Poor lad, everything is difficult for him. I don't want him to become a criminal." Once again he brushed his hair back and examined me distrustfully, and a hint of a smile spread across his face.

There is no choice, uncomfortable questions must be posed, any social worker knows that. "Does he want to work? If I find him job, will he take it?" Though my tone was very compassionate, attempting to soften the potential insult, he stood up, his face reddening, tossed down the cigarette butt he was holding, and shouted: "What do you think, that I come here for no reason? Because I have nothing to do? I told you, he needs a job! He already hangs around with criminals—"

"Please, sit down, take it easy, I didn't mean..."

His voice became louder, filling the office.

"What didn't you mean? What? I'm not an idiot. I know that's what you think, but I am not. You don't understand how difficult it is to raise children like that. You think everyone can afford a nanny, a cleaning lady, private lessons, like you? We could hardly feed the kids. You know who took care of them? They cared for each other. Yes, the older brother and sister looked after the youngsters! No one is there to help us, do you get it? And you ask if he will take the job, ha!"

His long body bent forward, and with a sharp and unexpected movement he ran his hand across the table, sweeping the papers and files off the desk, spreading them all over the room. He then rushed to the exit, cursing me in a loud shrill voice. As he ran down the stairs his curses could still be heard clearly, and only as he left the building did they fade away.

As I drove home I felt I could still hear the swearing and shouting, but the words and sentences were mixed and unclear. His home spread in my mind, neglect, dirty nappies on the floor, a ten-year-old girl feeding a toddler, constant noise coming from the TV, peeling walls, a simple loaf of bread on the kitchen table. I thought I could almost feel its stench. I did manage to find the son a proper job and called him to provide the details. He wrote them down and thanked me, with clear despair, "Maybe things will work out, I don't know, I hope I can hang in there."

Ruhama opened the door with Tomer in her arms. His eyes were red from crying, but as he saw me a huge smile spread across his face and he reached out for me.

"Sweetie, I've missed you," I mumbled as I carried him home; I almost said, "Mummy isn't leaving you now"—but suddenly the words seemed so insipid, even insulting, so I only kissed the soft cheek, and he hugged me as hard as he could, burying his face in the back of my neck, clinging to me desperately.

*

This morning, as I said goodbye to Tomer, I told myself that today I would be brave. In the afternoon, when I meet with Mr. Schuster, I would raise the possibility. And even if he looked at me with his watery eyes and waved his hand, I would insist and wouldn't let it go. In this early morning hour, as I held Tomer in my arms he leaned his head against my chest, peaceful and sleepy, he opened his eyes while dreaming, observed me bewilderedly and then fell asleep again, I swore not to give up. His feet popped out of the blue pyjamas, his hands held the buttons of my shirt unintentionally, his head was leaning back slightly, his mouth open, and his body had the scent of sweet sleep.

I love the early morning hours. I get up before dawn, make myself a cup of coffee, sit by the kitchen window and stare outside. The charm of the street at this hour is that nothing happens. Though the eye is automatically searching for movement, an unexpected event, everything is quiet and motionless. The rusty gutter of the house across the street, cars covered with dew, light mildew spreading between the stones of the fence around the building—and stillness. Sometimes a cat crosses the street, a bird flies and lands on a thin branch, but normally I enjoy the undisturbed street. It's calming and creates a sense of stability; the night is gone, there is no knowing what took place during the darkness, but in the early morning it turns out that everything has been left unchanged.

But since Tomer was born my mornings are not the same.

Already as I am staring at the street, the moment I will leave the house begins to materialize in my mind, and the feeling of stability I enjoy so much is undermined. Soon I will hear a rustle coming from Tomer's bed, he is moving in his sleep, sometimes touching the bed frame or a soft toy, emitting a weak *moo* or an almost soundless chirp. I ignore it, I keep looking out at the street, but then a little whimper is heard, a sort of grumble that the night's sleep is over and light begins to fill the room. I find him standing in bed, stretching his hands towards me though his eyes are still closed. When we sit down on the broad couch and I place the bottle in his mouth he drinks it without opening his eyes. Thin white drops cover his round mouth, dripping slowly onto his perfect chin, and I wipe it with a small towel.

Daphne is still fast asleep. I walk into the bedroom to grab a clean nappy and see her long body covered with a heavy winter blanket. Her face is sunk into the pillow, but from the top of the blanket a mane of long red hair is flowing, falling almost to the floor. The windows are closed. Her scent spreads in the room, and I realize that she and Tomer have a very similar smell: the fair skin and red hair have a cool milky perfume. When Daphne gets up she takes very small steps to the kitchen and then sits beside me, as Tomer opens his eyes, looking at his mother, stretching a hand towards her, revealing their intimacy.

Finally the moment comes when I need to get up, wash and shave, put on an ironed shirt and trousers and go to work. Tomer looks at me as I stand at the door. I have shed the pleasant fatherly appearance and assumed a respectable, serious one, which Tomer has started to dislike in the last couple of weeks. As I lean forward to kiss him he turns his head away and tightens his lips, showing that he has no intention of kissing me when I am elegantly dressed.

Daphne tried to persuade me to give up, not to attempt to kiss him before I go. "What does it matter, he doesn't like it that you look like that, when you return home and change he'll hug you and won't let go." But when she realized I insist on getting a kiss she left us alone. A minor insult created at the beginning of the day lingers until the evening (though it may appear to have been forgotten). I want him to put his moist lips on my lips and make a loud sound of a kiss in spite of the fact that I am about to leave the house and not return until in the evening. He refuses, turning his back on me and his baby face stubborn. Sometimes he crosses his arms, to prove that he isn't going to change his mind.

This morning I decided not to kiss him. Ashamed of feeling insulted, of considering myself rejected all through the day, a silly urge made me decide this. Before I went to work I said loudly, "Goodbye Tomer", kissed Daphne and left. I closed the door behind me and stood motionless, almost breathless, listening to voices coming from my home. At first there was silence. Then I heard mumbling, Daphne's voice mixed with Tomer's, and then he burst into tears, crying and gasping, making long piercing sobs.

Miserable. Miserable, you are so miserable, I said to myself, listening to your son cry, punishing him only to erase a ridiculous insult, a baby angry at his father when he is about to leave him from morning to night. But in spite of the insults I hurled at myself, I stood there until the sobbing faded away, admitting to myself that not only does Tomer need me, but I also need him.

Oddly, acknowledging such a simple and trivial thing made me feel better. On the way to work I kept repeating what I would say to Mr. Schuster, how I would explain my situation, elaborate on how my family members feel, describe what I think is the right solution, which would benefit everyone (mainly the firm). When I arrived at the office I immediately called his secretary and asked for an appointment. Ever since I had become one of his favourite accountants she approaches me speaking very quietly, at times I can hardly hear what she is saying. He is not in the office now, a whisper came from the phone, he is in a meeting, but as soon as he returns she would let him know I wanted to meet him. Yes, a personal matter, she won't forget to mention it.

I opened the window a crack; the rain-saturated air was so pleasant. I turned to the computer, placed several receipts in front of me, from the smallest amount to the largest, careful not to make a mistake. I always have red and blue pens beside me (I like to mark items, to avoid future mistakes). A cup of coffee was steaming beside me, the table lamp shed a pleasant light on the desk, and I was about to begin my work when a curvy feminine shadow was cast on the door.

"Amir, what's up? I haven't seen you for a while. I need some details on the Schneiderman-Cohen file."

Michelle, an astute accountant, frightening to many of the men in the office, stood at the door. A beautiful woman, everyone is intimidated by her very tight dresses, the flowing hair, a cleavage that generates embarrassment, high-heeled shoes (and impudent eyes that never ever look down). A colleague once told me she stands so close to men that they can feel her breathe. But her sharp tongue ridicules anyone who dares to criticize her demeanour. Strangely, she was nice to me. She came in and sat next to me, smiling, inquiring about the Schneiderman-Cohen file.

I am not sure why but her presence made me panic. Though unlike her usual self she sat casually and relaxed, her back leaning heavily against the backrest and her long legs stretched out, an obscure fear began to materialize, almost without me being aware of it. My thoughts, mixing with the professional discussion, were both excited and intimidated. What would happen if she sat closer to me?

"Schneiderman-Cohen really did spend too much this year, thus it will be hard to present a balanced picture."

I have heard that sometimes she touches men with her long nails, in a nonchalant manner, and they are left breathless.

"But I will do whatever I can to counterbalance the expenses."

Michelle listened patiently. Sometimes a smile flickered in her eyes, but then it faded and disappeared. Immersed in the details of the balance, she seemed indifferent to my uneasy movements, my confused answers, my avoiding looking straight into her eyes. I was drawn into a turbulence of anxiety that got fiercer as I contemplated an imaginary and unlikely scenario: if Michelle was to move closer, lean forward and touch my arm, I could neither withdraw nor stay still; if she smiles at me and suggests we meet after work, I will refuse, but my blushing face would reveal how sorry I am to refuse. Maybe I won't refuse, make all men in the office envious. Maybe she, like Sari, has a spacious modern flat in the centre of Tel Aviv? Or on a high floor in a tower overlooking the sea? And would the smell of her bed eventually become repulsive? And would her body, that now looks so attractive under the black dress, become distastefully familiar?

"Michelle, I would love to help you with this, but I need to make an urgent phone call," I heard myself saying.

With untypical kindness she apologized, she didn't know it would take so long. Please, could I email her the relevant details? As soon as she left the room I called Daphne.

"Hi, what's up? How is Tomer doing?"

"He's fine. Is everything okay? You sound a bit troubled."

"No. I was simply worried about Tomer, I heard him crying in the morning and I wanted to make sure everything was fine."

"Yeah, he's okay. He was already smiling as we got to Ruhama's, and he sat gladly on her lap."

"How is work?"

"All right. Hectic. Amir, is everything okay?"

"Yes. The truth is that, I don't know, suddenly I miss you."

"That's nice to hear. Maybe you could come home early today, and if it doesn't rain we could take Tomer for a walk in the park?"

"Wonderful. Great idea."

A gust of invigorating fresh air blew into the room, making the window tremble slightly. A scent of soil, of clear raindrops, and dry leaves filled the room. I was relieved. I suddenly thought of my father, who once in a while would lean back and emit a sigh of relief, illustrating not only with his voice but with his body how a concern was solved. In an instant he would fall back on the back rest, sometimes stretching his legs on the old footstool. If I were sure no one could see me I would place my feet on my desk.

A crack opened right next to me; thin and almost invisible. If I stepped on it, a chasm would be created, and I would fall down and hit the bottom with a thud. But I managed to leap over it, as if I didn't know how dangerous it could be, and took a step to the other side. I thought of Tomer's face as he rattled a small teddy bear, listening to the broken sound it makes, bursting into laughter, his cheeks rosy and full, his big eyes shining. Now I will work hard, skip lunch break, and return home early in the afternoon. By then the rain may stop, and Daphne and I will take a walk in the park. I will push the light stroller, she will hold my arm, and together we will smile at Tomer, wrapped in a bright red, winter coat.

I returned happily to work, delving into the expenditures and incomes of Schneiderman-Cohen. A smart accountant has interesting insights into people in the firm, simply by looking at the balance sheet. One partner spends too much on dining in fancy restaurants, the other asks to be reimbursed for unnecessary business travels. Also strange spending on stationery, cleaning, transportation—any innocent-looking article may conceal a minor theft. An accountant must calculate his steps wisely: not to inquire too much but to maintain an acceptable balance, not to change too much but abide by the law. I looked into some unclear figures, added numbers, sometimes checking the regulations. After a couple of hours I was exhausted and took a break. Years of experience had taught me that with the first confusion, when I am suddenly not sure what figure goes where, I should let go. It would be foolish to continue, it will only create double work, correcting mistakes that generate more mistakes, calculations that are sometimes lost in a body of numbers I can't figure out anymore.

I leaned back, closed my eyes and breathed in the moist air, inhaling water vapours, condensing and becoming sky, before falling back to the ground. Yesterday Daphne's body stretched on the bed, her eyes closed, the breasts so heavy that they slide to the side, a belly embroidered with thin, delicate silver stripes, legs tightly crossed.

A woman who evokes the right sort of passion, as though

if I sink into her I would reach the bottom of the earth.

As I caressed her she opened her eyes and drew me to her. Still, as I dropped into her arms, bewilderment was mixed with the pleasure. Ever since Tomer was born we always hear him breathe, even when he is fast asleep in his room. An out of sight baby's rustle follows us constantly, even when we don't want to hear it. But the short, quick breath cannot be silenced, this sound of a small body in bed, the whispering a soft toy makes even though it's untouched. And now this obscure swish blends with our naked bodies lying on the bed, blunting a desirable sharpness, a certain needed distance between a man and a woman, replacing it with a mutual alertness to the sound of movement coming from the next room.

A phone call brought me back to the office at once. My body, relaxed on the swivel chair, became tense and alert. I tucked my shirt back into my trousers, and only then I picked up the phone. In twenty minutes Mr. Schuster will be available. He wants to know how the Schneiderman-Cohen case is coming along. Yes, he is aware that it is about a personal matter, still, he asks that I bring some documents.

As I came into his office Mr. Schuster was on the phone. Someone on the other end of the line was making him very angry. He listened and once in a while said, "nonsense, I simply can't understand how you say this," as he turned his fountain pen from side to side, his face betraying utter disgust. A squeaky male voice came from the phone. I couldn't understand what he was saying, but Mr. Schuster's pen moved faster and faster, until he almost dropped it. "Listen, there is no point in having this conversation. If you want to talk, say something that makes some sense," he said loudly, and the squeaks from the other end also became louder.

I sat down facing him, placing my papers on the desk, waiting for the call to end. This anger might not be good for me, I thought (maybe I should please him with work before we talk about me). I will show him how much progress I have made on the Schneiderman-Cohen case, and only then will I turn to personal issues.

When the call was finally over he looked at me as if he had just discovered I was in the room. He said nothing of the squeaky voice coming from the phone, only sighed sullenly and asked me what it was that I wanted to talk about. I spread the papers out on the desk, a variety of tables and diagrams indicating how the annual statement of such a huge company was progressing. I spoke rapidly, explaining my decisions simply and eloquently, how they created an accurate and balanced picture, moving quickly from one diagram to another, as Mr. Schuster tried to follow me. After a couple of minutes he seemed a bit confused. When I was convinced the anger had dissipated I put down my pen and said I would like to discuss something else, an issue that is personal yet which may affect the firm.

Mr. Schuster leaned back, folded his arms in an authoritative manner, placed them on his protruding belly, and observed me sceptically. An experienced and accomplished manager, nothing raises his suspicion like an employee claiming that what is good for him is useful for the firm. More than once I have heard him say that employees want to go home and the boss wants them to work, that's how the world is. His watery eyes were wide open now, almost as though he was in a dark room, unable to see who is facing him. A blank and impartial gaze, he was waiting for me to explain myself.

"I am sure you remember my son was born about a year

ago. Until recently my wife stayed at home, but now she has gone back to work. He is with a caregiver for many hours, I hardly see him during weekdays, only in the evening. I would very much like to take part in caring for him, it is very important for me. I would like to suggest, and I hope you would agree, that two days a week I will come late to the office, perhaps early afternoon, and then work late into the night. I am a dedicated accountant, I hope you agree, I put all my efforts into work, I manage to complete very complex cases quicker than anyone else here. And if I do not keep on schedule, I pledge to finish the work on weekends. I am sure I will work much faster in the evenings when it is very quiet here, and I could get more work done."

A glimmer of mockery, almost invisible, flashed in his watery eyes, and gradually developed and spread on his face. "Why is it that you think that you will get more work done in the evening?"

"Because I need complete silence to work. And during work hours there is always a certain bustle, someone is always distracting me."

"Tell me who is interrupting you."

"No one is interrupting me on purpose. It is just that there are people around."

"And you say you will work when you will be here alone at night?"

"Yes."

Mr. Schuster chuckled, and then stopped.

"And how exactly will I know that you are working?"

"When you see how much I accomplish you will have no doubt what I am doing when I am in my office."

Again a noise like a chuckle came out of his mouth.

"But you already accomplish a lot, so how exactly would

it be useful to me if you come when no one else is here? On the contrary, it can only slow you down."

He seemed slightly bemused, as if this was a theoretical discussion and I, the young man, was unable to reply to the old professor's questions. He couldn't see my trepidation (the very detailed portrayal of my life), the deep desire to raise my son, or maybe he didn't want to acknowledge them. What has he got to do with the wishes of a young accountant? The firm needs to succeed, to flourish, he wants to have new clients, and this won't happen if he doesn't make sure that the accountants are fully committed to work.

"Amir, I want you to know that denying your request is for your own good. You don't understand this, but it's true."

"How is it for my own good?"

"I make sure you make a living. If you and others here aren't fully committed to work I will lose clients, and I would have to fire some of you."

"I understand this. As I've said, I will work as much as I do now, only at different hours."

"There is no such thing. Accountants work only when someone is watching them. No one likes to make calculations all day long. It's work. And if you are here alone late in the evening gradually you will stop, because no one is making you work. In the morning you will say you didn't manage to complete what you planned."

"I promise it won't be like that. Every morning I'll show you what I've done the previous night."

"Believe me, nothing would be done. I also raised my children this way. My wife took care of them, and I saw them late in the evening and on weekends. That's the way it is. If you want to make money you need to be here during working hours."

"I want to take part in raising my son."

Fury flashed in the watery eyes. He put the pen on the desk, stood up, and said in a loud voice without looking down at me: "If you want to stay with us you must be here during working hours. If it doesn't suit you, please, you're free to go. I must say you disappoint me. You are very gifted, I was going to appoint you head of a department, but now I see you're not as serious as I thought you were." He then waved his hand in his usual manner, but this time it was clear it was meant to make me leave his office.

I took the stairs and not the lift to hide my tears. Tomer, my love, my boy, the recollection of the fresh baby scent made me sit on the stairs and weep. I buried my face in my hands to conceal my sobbing. The dim light in the stairway and the heavy air made me nauseous. In a minute I would have stepped out to the street and never returned to the firm. But after a couple of minutes I stood up, tucked my shirt into my trousers, brushed off the dust and went down the stairs to my office, my heart tormented with pain and fury, as though fatherhood had been stolen from me.

Twenty-First Month

Desert wind in mid-winter creates turmoil in nature. Clouds are dusty, heavy and lacking fragility, a film of sand wraps the trees, yellow light infiltrates the grey sky, and a glance at the sea reveals the end of the world at the horizon. The beauty of the sea dissipates when sky is heavier than water. I sit here, on my mother's balcony, watching the grey sea and the huge sky enveloping us, smiling, and my heart pounds rapidly.

Guy.

In a couple of minutes the buyer will come. A widower, a banker from Haifa who retired recently and wants to live in Tel Aviv. He came twice to see the apartment, pacing from one room to another, opening and closing windows and blinds, asking peculiar questions: How high is the room? What are the windows' hinges made of? How big are the two bathrooms together? I told him I am an interior decorator, hoping to evade his questions, suggesting that they are pointless, but he didn't give up. On the contrary, once he learned of my profession he began to inquire about various materials. I found his questions so exhausting that finally I interrupted him and apologized, I am sorry, I need to make an urgent phone call, I will be right back.

A week after his second visit he called to say he decided he wants the apartment. I told my mother, and she said: "Abigail, you take care of all this. If you wish, you can live there. If not, you determine what the right price is. I'll accept any decision you make." I wasn't sure whether I should take the banker's offer. I didn't even consider living there, but maybe I could have gotten a higher price for such an elegant place, on a high floor in a tower facing the sea. But the urge to flee this house made me take his offer. Mum and I have lived here for years; life was peaceful and comfortable, but always touched by sadness. The elegant appearance covered a certain dreariness, which I had no desire to maintain. And neither did Mum.

Since I won the prize she has changed. New clients congratulate me for winning but emphasize that they want a "modern," "contemporary" home, one that would express the present-day spirit of Tel Aviv. But not Mum. After she saw the apartment that won me the prestigious prize she began to rummage through her drawers and pulled out things she had kept for years: a picture of the three of us in an old fashioned gilded wooden frame, a handmade tablecloth embroidered with tiny animals, an old coffee set, and more and more and more. As she looked at them her face completely changed, taking on an unfamiliar expression. Normally her sadness blended with a tranquil countenance, typical of wealthy women; now her wide-open eyes betrayed naked pain. They were often filled with tears. She would place the old objects somewhere and sink into the huge armchair facing the sea, with eyes closed. Once in a while she would tell me more about our life before Dad died, but I could tell she was trying to cut it short, not to turn the past into a burden.

Where is Guy?

Four months ago, one evening in the fall, I joined her for dinner. I was working on the renovation of an apartment two blocks away from her. At seven o'clock, after hours of hard work, I was tired and hungry, and decided that rather than drive to my home and order food, I would walk to the tall tower overlooking the sea. I could almost smell the delicacies she would pull out of the fridge, and hunger made me walk briskly against the breeze coming from the sea.

Mum was happy to see me, but a small muscle in her face tensed as she invited me to come in. Her eyes, which had completely lost the expression of constant comfort, were wide open, revealed happiness with an unfamiliar panic. I rushed to the fridge, eager to satisfy my hunger, but I suddenly realized that someone was standing in the kitchen—maybe coming to fix something, I thought, a plumber or a repairman. A big man about fifty years old, with long grey hair and prominent facial features: dark eyes, a flat-tipped and fleshy nose, full lips. His blue jeans seemed messy, the red and black plaid flannel shirt was worn. But to my utter surprise Mum said, "Come, why don't you join Saul and me for dinner."

Immediately she turned her back on me so that I couldn't see her expression, and Saul sat at the table and began to eat without waiting for us to join him.

The cord binding and connecting us together was stretched to its limit and cut. I have never seen Mum's eyes like this, alive and scared, full of pleasure and embarrassment. She looked at me, waiting for my response, and I just stood there, frozen. A thin smile came across her face and she sat down at the table, and so did I. I couldn't eat a thing. The hunger was gone. A mild pain prevented me from touching the variety of sausages and cheeses she offered.

In a moment our shared tranquillity was shattered. Years of a comfortable life blended with melancholy, a two-person family with no urge to grow and embrace others, always knowing that the past was better than the present— and suddenly the walls around us had been breached. Mum invited a strange man, big and unrefined, home and she was asking me to join them for dinner.

After a little while I took my leave. I decided to walk home. A mixture of cold air and dust painted the sky with red undertones, the moon was surrounded by an opaque halo. I walked for half an hour, repeating the words I had just heard as though they were in a language unknown to me: "A friend of mine, owner of a fabric shop in south Tel Aviv, I came to order fabric to reupholster the sofa, about two months ago, will you have something? I thought you were hungry." The bulky masculine hands broke the cheese, tore huge slices of bread, the dark eyes looked at me with suspicion and followed Mum's face and body shamelessly. As I got home I dropped on the bed, with my clothes and jacket on, and fell asleep until the morning.

When will Guy call?

Mum left the flat. She bought a smaller one in the centre of Tel Aviv, in an old building with a slightly mouldy stairwell. When I offered to renovate it she smiled and simply said, "I don't want it renovated. I want it exactly as it is." She and Saul spend hours together, talking in a way only they understand. Every Friday night she invites me to dine with them, but only rarely do I go.

I was completely engaged with work. The prize brought many clients, now also municipalities approached me, asking me to design public spaces. A life of toil, from morning to evening, illustrations, sketches, textures, the balance between light and shade, satisfaction filled me as I watched my ideas materialize, transforming ordinary, sometimes ugly, places into pleasant and comfortable spaces. One municipality asked me to renovate a school for disabled children. The budget was negligible. The children's cheers, walking with crutches or sitting in wheelchairs, as they saw their school become appealing brought me to tears. One girl, about five years old, approached me limping, and as she stood right next to me she asked, "Did you make all this?"

"Yes," I answered, and she craned her neck forward with an effort and kissed my cheek.

I became self-absorbed, retrieving from within me combinations of colours and shapes I never knew existed. I hardly saw Mum, only rarely went out with friends, I was completely consumed by fabric, wood, plastic, glass, insulation materials, gardens. From an obscure place new ideas emerged. I found a huge space existing within me, a labyrinth leading to surprising avenues. People, places, anything I saw disintegrated into splotches of colour and angles that then combined into new shapes.

When I finished renovating the school for disabled children, exhaustion overtook me. I rushed home, went into the bathroom, took off the high-heeled shoes and the black shirt and trousers. The mascara, eye shadow, lipstick and foundation created colourful spots on the white wipe. I was standing facing the mirror, drained but peaceful, looking with a pleasant distance at the reflection of my body in the huge mirror. Nice feet, feminine legs, wide feminine hips that grow into a thin chest with virginal breasts; a small curved mermaid. I looked straight into the mirror, directly into my eyes. A flicker of laughter emerged and disappeared, replaced by a spark of new, unfamiliar light, writhing within me and then breaking out, a hint of rebirth, after which one can drop one's head onto the pillow, lie in bed, and fully relax.

When Guy showed up at my door in the evening two days ago, ringing the bell and standing there like an embarrassed child, I felt as if a heavy weight had dropped from the upper part of my body. We haven't been in touch for a couple of months. I always carried something of his presence within me, a memory of a familiar body odour, but I got used to his absence. After we broke up, I often thought I saw him on the street, but when I returned from London I was inundated with work, and the distress slowly faded and was replaced by tranquillity. Daphne's pregnancy and Tomer's birth were no longer part of me. Every time I thought about it, after a couple of moments something became blurred, a complication that not only could not be purged but also generated further confusion. Strollers are so ugly, daddy didn't want another child, Guy expressed no interest in children before Daphne got pregnant, I wonder what would be the best way to design a child's room, Mum spends so much time with Saul, it all merged into one thought, lengthy and continuous, that always ended in the principles of home design or new materials that I could use, and I'm glad it did. The conclusion of this twisting thought was often cheerful.

But when Guy stood at the door, staring at me, the tranquillity of the last months vanished at once. The sight of his face, somewhat pale in the winter, and the crown of curls on his head was overwhelming. Two small wrinkles, fine lines granting his masculine face a thoughtful countenance appeared between the green eyes. Strange, but a feeling of anxiety, sharp and quick, washed over me as I saw the two wrinkles, as if I could witness him getting old in an instant. In a minute he would bend down, develop a hump, and his face would take on a bitter, grumpy expression. I leaned on the doorframe, unable to decide what to do, hug him or invite him politely to come in. As I stretched my arms towards him he grabbed me, embracing me so strongly I could hardly breathe. A man and a woman clinging to each other, inhaling familiar scents, a smooth neck, the curls a bit stiff, stubble, wide chest, and finally taking a step back. There is no need for him to tell me how much he's missed me, his eyes shine with a mixture of joy and pain, he follows my gaze, trying to catch my eye, but I bury my face in his body. An unfamiliar shiver shakes the arms around me, a determined and unequivocal touch, a gesture of yearning.

"Abigail, I've missed you so much."

"Guy, I—"

"Come, let me kiss you. Where have you been all this time?"

"Here. In London. Here. I don't know."

"My love, come here…"

I move back, pushing him way, tearing myself away from the strong arms.

"No, I don't want this. It took me so long to get over you, you know… I can't go through this again. Breaking up was so hard, but now I finally feel good again."

"Listen, you don't understand—"

"I understand everything. I won't change. I don't want

children. I don't have a motherly instinct, a need to be a mother. I wish I could change it, but it is impossible. This is who I am, and that's it. I don't fully understand it myself, but it can't be changed."

"I know."

"My mum says I am like my dad, he was like that."

"I didn't know that."

"I am absorbed by work, enjoying every minute of it, nothing is lacking in my life."

"I know you always look around you."

"It is a gaze directed inwards, not outwards. Everything I see becomes an object that I then use in designing. It is an attention to myself, not to others. Maybe this is preventing me from being a mother. Mothers are always looking at other people, I look at myself."

"I am not sure. Some mothers have flourishing careers."

"I don't know what is right for others, only for myself. I don't want children and I am certain it won't change. And I also understand how important it is for you to be a father."

"True. It is important. But I guess there are things more important than that."

"What do you mean?"

"Abigail, I want you."

"I don't want to deprive you of fatherhood. And I don't want to live with a man who always wants something I'm unable to give."

"Abigail, I am here to stay. I am not going anywhere."

"But how will we manage?"

"I have no idea. Even if you wanted to have children, no one knows what would have happened. Come closer, let me hold you, rest your head on my shoulder, my love."

＊

"Hey, Abrahami, how are you? I haven't seen you in ages."

"Guy, what's up? It's been years since we last met."

"Yes, time flies. How are you? Do you still own the garage?"

"Yeah, it's going really well. Big business now! Why don't you bring your car in for a service?"

"Good idea. I need to fix a water leak in my car. Anyway, how are you? What are you doing here?"

"Ah, my ex-wife lives here. I came to fetch my daughter."

"I'm sorry, I didn't know you were divorced. When did this happen?"

"Three years ago. I got to tell you, it's a messy thing."

"Why?"

"Well, you know, we fight about money. And also we have a daughter. She is five years old now."

"Many people divorce these days. Children adjust eventually."

"Yeah, but they suffer. Anyone who says it isn't so isn't telling the truth. Sometimes I am sorry we had her."

"What?"

"Don't get me wrong, I'm crazy about her, I'll do anything for her, but it makes everything so complicated."

"I'm sure it will work out! My parents got divorced. I went through a tough time, but I got used to it."

"Ah, I don't know. What do you mean 'got used'? Honestly, I don't get it."

"It was different for me. I stayed with my mum, and my dad left us. I saw him very rarely."

"So you got used to living without your dad?"

"Yes. Sort of."

"I don't understand why people still get married these days. You know, in the past everything was about family, people got married and had kids. But if it isn't for that, who needs it?"

"Most people want to have a family, but they don't always succeed."

"You aren't married, are you?"

"No."

"So why get married? It's useless. The way you look, I bet lots of women want you, you can fuck around, why commit to one woman?"

"Well…"

"And if you get married and have children, they suffer terribly if you divorce. My daughter asks me if I will leave her the way I left mom. It kills me."

"…"

"You said you broke up with your girlfriend, did you? Why?"

"Because she won't have children."

"What, is she infertile? Poor woman."

"No, she doesn't want children."

"How can that be possible? It's against a woman's nature."

"That's how she feels. She loves her work and doesn't want to be a mother."

"I don't get it. Every woman wants to be a mother."

"She doesn't."

"Frankly, no offence, don't get me wrong, but I think it's good you broke up. There is probably something wrong with her—"

"Excuse me?"

"I'm sure she looks great and everything, a successful

woman, but don't you think she is a bit screwed up if she doesn't want kids? C'mon, don't lie. I don't mean to offend or anything, but it's unnatural. Women want children."

"Abrahami, we're not the Middle Ages, you know."

"Since you left her, obviously you feel the same!"

"No, I left her because I want to be a father, not because I think there is something wrong with her."

"Oh, c'mon, admit it: you think she's messed up."

"Forget it. It's private. Everything is fine with her. I mean, everyone has something wrong, so what? People aren't perfect. Neither are you, you know. That's life."

"Oh, you're so modern. 'People aren't perfect,' well done. That's bullshit. There are men, women and children, that's it. If you didn't think the same you'd still be with her."

"For a person who's recently divorced, you're pretty confident! Here, you married and had a daughter, and now you're on your way to your ex-wife, to spend a couple of hours with your daughter."

"Stop it, Guy, don't be angry with me. I meant no harm."

"Wouldn't it be better if your ex-wife hadn't wanted children? Didn't you just say you're sorry you had your daughter?"

"Never mind, forget it. Don't freak out. Everyone does what's right for him or her."

"Sometimes the problem is that people don't do what is right for them."

"Never mind. How did we get into this? How is it going at work?"

"I've got to go."

A soft autumn sun illuminates the street, a pleasant wind caresses my cheeks and neck, dry leaves circle in the air and fall on empty street benches. The beauty of the street is tainted by Abrahami's words. He finds everything so simple and clear, the natural path and the human condition, and if he encounters a different, peculiar inclination, a rare desire, rhyming words, he immediately finds faults, declares failure, condemns and excludes.

A strange idea is gradually materializing: I'll go to the sea now, early in the afternoon. I won't run along the coast but sit facing the water, looking forward, relaxing on one of the deckchairs on the beach, staring only at foam, water, sky. And when Abrahami's claims lose their sting and turn into empty words I'll walk into the water. I'll step forward slowly until I am fully submerged in the sea, obscure currents will embrace my body, salty water will clean it, penetrating into every corner, leaving it fresh and pure, and then I'll come out of the sea, open my eyes like a newborn after birth, and propose to Abigail.

Tomer is One Year Old

One step after another. The small body is slightly wobbly, making an effort to maintain stability, but the desire to walk causes Tomer to grip my hand tightly and totter on. Wearing a red jacket with gold buttons, a colourful hat, shiny brand new blue shoes; he and I walk on the promenade along the seashore in the afternoon, on a pleasant cloudy winter day. When I think he is tired I suggest that he sit in the stroller, but he shrugs in a deliberate manner and says "_o."

I left the welfare office early today so that I could take Tomer to the beach. As I drove from the center of Tel Aviv to the sea I wondered what the shore would look like: every day a different picture is drawn on the huge canvas spreading from the shore to the horizon, and then to the sky. Endless shapes and colors, an artist's hand that never, ever repeats itself, constantly pouring a fresh mix onto the picture, creating new tones and patterns that blend together. Today it stretched a strip of soft clouds upon the sky, concealing the sun but allowing its soft rays to permeate, plunge to the water and create orange pink stains on the sea.

Later today the family will come to celebrate Tomer's first birthday, but now only the two of us are here, mother and child, holding hands, taking one step after another, breathing air saturated with salt, gazing at the sea. A black dog leaps on the shore. When Tomer sees him he cries joyfully "_og, _og." The dog walks into the water, stands still, bewildered, watching the waves, and then charges back onto the sand.

Last night Amir stroked my hair and said, "Daphne, what do you say we have another child?" Lying in bed, exhausted after a long day, the TV flickered and murmured in our bedroom, the sound of Tomer's breathing came from his room, and we were almost asleep. But the very moment these words were articulated, innocent and loving, the bubble within me contracted in an instant. I closed my eyes, surrendering to the movement of his fingers on my forehead, clinging to the sensation with the hope that it would remove the fear, vanquish the panic spreading quickly as I heard the words "another child". As I was hesitating how to respond the fingers stopped moving, and the sound of Amir's breathing as he slept filled the room. I got up and went into the kitchen. I had two biscuits left on the table, and some orange juice; I peeled a banana and ate it hastily, and finally stuck a finger into the jam and licked all of it. I then folded Tomer's clothes, and finally washed two dishes left in the sink. But it was useless.

I went into Tomer's room to watch him sleep. I tiptoed in, standing by the bed and looking at him lying on his back, his head surrounded by red curls, a high forehead, freckles on his nose, his mouth slightly open, his body lax in sleep. Whenever I watch him asleep great happiness blends with the frailty created by the labour. And now the fear, that had disappeared since the delivery, had been reawakened. I kissed his cheek and he moved his hand in his asleep, wishing to push away the unwanted intruder.

"_ma, _ma," Tomer stretches his hands towards me, tired now from walking. I pick him up and put him in the stroller, and he doesn't resist. Worn out, he snatches the bottle I hand him and gulps the water. The movement of the stroller makes him fall asleep. After a couple of minutes I see his head reclined back, his eyes closed and his cheeks rosy from the sea air. Today at lunch, Rotem asked me what it was like to be a mother, now that it's been a year. Gal smiled at me, nibbling the Indian food she had for lunch, and said: "Well, Daphne, it's true that after the child is born everything is different, isn't it?"

"Different? Yes, absolutely."

Rotem's eyes were wide as she asked me to elaborate. "I'm not sure how to describe it. After Tomer was born everything changed. I now find my previous thoughts rather funny." Rotem's blue eyes were shining. Her desire to understand what Gal and I were talking about made her look childlike, as though she were trying to discover a secret kept from children. She asked, "What, is it like the last piece of a jigsaw puzzle? Something that makes you feel like a whole person?"

I hesitated but Gal responded, "Well, it's the last piece of a jigsaw puzzle, but when you put it in its proper place it doesn't produce the picture you expect, but rather a completely different one."

Rotem's eyes were curious, attentive to what Gal was saying. After a moment of silence she said, "Then why don't you have more children? When I get married I want to have five children."

Smiling, Gal looked at her, her face betraying her kindness, and responded quietly, "The picture is completely different from what I imagined it would be, but this new one has flaws I never knew existed."

"What do you mean?" Rotem asked, and Gal answered in a low voice, "I didn't know that my self-perception would change. That I'd see myself as a different person. I know it sounds strange, but still…"

They kept talking and I became oblivious. I saw Gal talking as she ate and Rotem washing the dishes in the office's small kitchen, yet I found it difficult to follow the conversation. A nice cloudy day, I thought, I could take Tomer to the beach. I am glad it isn't raining, I need to make a cake for tonight, clean the house. I heard Gal saying, "it's enough to go through this once," but her words were drowned in a stream of disconnected thoughts. If I leave the office two hours early I will be ahead of traffic and would get to Ruhama quickly, maybe I will first go by the grocery shop. In the evening Mum will surely have annoying comments, and Dad will tell her to stop it, I am not sure what I should wear, a tight dress that shows my slim figure, or perhaps something loose, more appropriate for a mother on her son's birthday? Without hearing what they were talking about, but with obscure agitation, I suddenly said out loud, almost shouting: "Rotem, you know what? We are throwing Tomer a birthday party tonight, and I feel I need to choose between looking attractive or motherly, and I find it rather strange. In the past I never had to make such choices."

They both looked at me, bewildered by my words, which I had blurted out almost against my will.

"Daphne, you look terrific, you don't need to worry about that…" said Rotem. Gal smiled.

"I know, I know, but that's beside the point. This feeling that I need to choose is distressing."

"You sound as if you were sorry you had a child."

"What?! No! Not at all! I'm happy with him every single

moment, Tomer fills me with joy. But you better be aware that the world is divided into women and mothers."

"I don't get it. Some mums look absolutely fantastic."

"That has nothing to do with it. It's an inner split."

Tomer wakes up. Soft sunbeams filter in between the clouds, tickling his closed eyes, and he blinks and opens them. More people are walking along the beach now, and once in a while I need to turn the stroller so as not to hit anyone. The clouds that cover the sky gradually part, allowing light falling from above to cast a transparent glare on the sea, which swallows it without leaving a trace. The water is heavy, humming and whistling, foaming and hurtling ahead, the sky is silent and motionless. The sea is material and vital, the sky is transparent and noble. My outburst at lunch when talking to Rotem is so distressing, I didn't want this inner voice to be heard. I didn't want the strange frailty spreading within me since the delivery to be seen. But it is taking root and is expanding. I never suspected that physical weakness would create self-doubt, excessive caution, fear of the unknown. And the folk wisdom—if you experience it once you won't be afraid anymore—turned out to be false, an illusion. Pain has only created a deeper fear.

Tomer turns around and smiles as me, pointing at a seagull flying over the sea. As he sees me immersed in thought he keeps staring at me, wondering why I don't share his amazement. I bend down to him to fondle his head. Suddenly he stretches his arms, grabs me and kisses my cheek. My eyes are filled with tears: my beloved Tomer, my son, I pick him up and hug him fervently, and holding him in my arms I walk to the sea, standing in the sand right next to the water. Low waves lick my feet but I don't care, Tomer and I are holding each other and staring at the sea. The blanket of clouds covering the sky disintegrated into small chunks, grey and soft, and from behind them the sun appears, descending slowly to the sea, a blazing fire nearing the water. The high waves die down, the sea is now vibrant and restless. Tomer puts his head on my shoulder, I can feel his baby breath, and so we stand motionless, tranquil and loving, waiting for the sun to set and for darkness to fill the earth.